THE NIGHT DADDY

The Night Daddy

by *MARIA GRIPE*

WITH DRAWINGS BY
Harald Gripe

Translated from the Swedish by
Gerry Bothmer

A YEARLING BOOK

THE NIGHT DADDY

JULIA

O.K. I'LL WRITE IT all by myself and then he can do what he likes. Besides, I've already started, although he doesn't know that. I began writing about us the second day he was here, but of course I didn't know that it would turn into a book.

That's what it's going to be because there are a lot of things no one will believe that I have to prove. It's very important.

I want him to work with me on this, but he doesn't want to. He says it's nobody's business that he's a night daddy. And that's true, but he's never met Ulla and the other kids in my class, and he has no idea what they're like. Otherwise he'd change his mind soon enough.

He says he wants it to be *our* secret, but that's not what *I* want. Grownups sometimes have such funny secrets that aren't really secrets at all, and sometimes they say a lot of things they don't mean because they don't want to be bothered with kids—they even try to pull the wool over their eyes.

My night daddy isn't like that, and although he is a bit on the lazy side, he does listen when I talk to him. He said that he doesn't have the time to write this book, but I know he does, because when he isn't reading he's writing. I told him so, and he said he had to, because it was his work and. . . .

He's writing a book about stones. Doesn't that sound weird? All the books he reads are also about stones. *Stones* that you throw and walk on—imagine people writing books about that!

When I told him that the book I'm writing is about us—him and me and Smuggler—he said that I couldn't do that. When you write about real people he says it's called a *roman à clef*, which means the reader knows exactly who the characters are.

But what difference does that make? I think it sounds like fun. O.K. "We'll write a *roman à clef*," I said. I had Ulla and the rest of the kids in mind.

"Otherwise they'll think I invented you—or else they'll say I'm dreaming."

I couldn't see his face because he had his back toward me and was looking out the window.

"Sometimes I feel just like an invention," he said.

"Then all you can do is what those who have invented you invent for you to do," I said. "And that can't be much fun."

But I do know what he means because sometimes when you come into a room where there are a lot of people, they just sit there gaping and waiting for you to say something funny, and you do feel like a stupid invention.

"O.K. Then I'd rather be a dream," he said.

"But that makes no sense at all! A dream can only be what the dreamer dreams," I said.

"But it could be fun if you're the dreamer. . . ."

When he talks like that I just don't know what to say. I don't remember what my answer was, but it will come back to me. Since my night daddy came, I remember things so much better than I used to. I don't think I've ever forgotten a single thing he said, what I've said to him, or anything we've ever done together. It's much more fun to remember things these days. Before he came hardly anything was worth remembering. The days went by, one by one, as in that old silly riddle—I mean the one about the clock that kept on running and never got as far as the door. The only thing I wanted to do then was just sit around and think my own thoughts. I still like to do that, but not all the time the way I used to.

"Why do you write about stones?"

He was always puffing on his pipe and blowing out smoke, which sometimes came out gray, sometimes blue, and sometimes almost yellow. He said the color depended on whether he was smoking dried lingonberry leaves, mint leaves, or a mixture.

"BECAUSE," he said.

He's learned that from me. That's what I say when I'm sure of the answer although I can't quite put it into words.

If you're so happy or sad about something that you can't think about anything else, but you don't want to keep on talking about it, it's a good idea to write it down. I'm writing this because I'm so happy, and also because I want Ulla and the other kids to know that I have a night daddy, and that I haven't made it up, which is what they seem to think.

Night daddies are *real* daddies, and I'm going to prove it!

I'm going to write this book at night when all is quiet and everyone is asleep, when he thinks I'm sleeping too—while he is in there writing about stones and listening to music—when the sky is dark except for the stars, that's when I'm going to write my book.

"But why does it have to be about us?" he asks.

"BECAUSE," I say.

THE NIGHT DADDY

"BECAUSE" said Julia, and that was that.

This could have been such a wonderful secret. Why couldn't we keep it to ourselves? I didn't want to tell a living soul—except for Smuggler, of course —that Julia was my night child and I her night daddy.

It was no one else's business, and besides, what was so strange about it? Since there were day mommies why shouldn't there be night daddies?

"That's right. And that's the reason we have to write about it," said Julia.

Julia has a way of twisting things around. "But I

like secrets," I said, trying to approach it from a different angle.

"I do, too," said Julia, "and that's why."

I didn't follow her, but she was quick to explain: I had a square approach to secrets, she said. Secrets were not so simple as people seemed to think. Things only became secrets when you began *talking* about them. Those are the *real* secrets.

Only the small and unimportant secrets seem to grow bigger if you bury them, but it only seems that way; it really isn't so at all.

Grownups like *little* secrets. But not Julia.

At first I thought that she was talking nonsense, but Julia thinks a lot—far more than I do—and she managed to explain it to me in a way that made sense.

"The secret of a real secret is that the more you talk about it, the more secret it becomes," she said. "You can keep on talking about it forever and it just keeps on growing, and the sharing of it is such fun. Then you realize just how much that secret is hiding. There's no end to it.

"To keep a secret like this to yourself is no good. It's even harmful," says Julia. "The more you choke it down, the more depressed you get. It shrivels up inside its silent dungeon, and you never know how important it was until it has vanished forever."

That's about the way Julia explained it to me, and I began to see that there was something to what she said. My approach to secrets had been square, but it isn't any longer. Now I know that they are just as complex and as strange as everything else in life.

Julia is as wise as an owl. One can learn a lot from her. She is also as stubborn as a mule.

When I was finally talked into writing this book with her, I tried to drag my feet. I didn't know exactly where to begin, and I wanted more time to think about it.

"We have to begin from the beginning, of course," said Julia.

"Yes, but I don't know when the beginning was," I tried to say. But she wasn't listening to a word I said and broke in:

"No one knows when things start and when they end," she remarked with her usual wisdom, "so we have to start from the very beginning. Now it's *your* turn."

"O.K." I said. (I often say that, and Julia has picked it up. O.K. was definitely not a part of her vocabulary when we first met.)

O.K. But I still can't figure out exactly when it all began. It must have been a long time ago, when I was looking for a place to live. It's hard to find a room around here; I made a lot of phone calls but people only sighed. "Maybe in ten years," they said.

Of course I could live in a tent, or in a trailer, or perhaps even on a houseboat? That would be marvelous! Imagine, just to drift along and then drop anchor whenever the spirit moved you! So I asked around about houseboats, but there didn't seem to be any for rent.

That's how I happened to meet Jansson.

"Well, now let's see," he said. He's a sea captain and knows all about boats. "What would the likes of you want with a houseboat?"

"I'd like to live on one," I said.

"Landlubbers ought to stay where they belong," he growled. "What's wrong with an ordinary house?"

"Nothing, except I can't seem to find one with a room for me."

"Then you can have mine," said Jansson, just like that.

All I could do was stare at him.

"I have to go to Gothenburg. Why should I leave it empty? You might as well move in."

That's the way I finally got a room. But Jansson didn't call it a room—he called it a "cabin."

When I moved in with my stuff, I realized exactly

what he meant. It was much too small to be called a room, and fitting my things in was a problem. I had to leave everything down in the courtyard and bring it up piece by piece and try to work it in like a puzzle. I managed to find space for a bed, a table, a bureau, a wicker chair, and a bookshelf on the wall. All the rest had to be stored in the attic. But that was all right. I really didn't need anything else. The books were a problem though. I'm writing a book—not Julia's and mine, but another one which I'm doing on my own.

It isn't a fairy tale or an adventure story or anything like that, but the kind that most people thumb through and say to themselves: "What a bore!" But then there are a few who read every word and say: "This is very interesting. . . . I didn't know that. . . ."

Those are the people for whom I'm writing this book. There are books about everything between heaven and earth, about birds and fishes, trees and flowers. . . .

My book is about stones—all kinds of stones. Why stones? I'll come to that later.

The word "stone" usually brings to mind the ordinary gray kind, but there are lots of beautiful and unusual stones that have beautiful and unusual names, as do flowers and birds. There is migmatite. There is hornblende—and dolomite and margarite, and porphyry, iron glance, hematite, tigereye and rock crystal.

There are lots and lots of them, one more beautiful than the other. People know hardly anything about stones. Anyway, in order to write this book, I have to read a lot of other books, and that's my big problem. The bookshelf on this wall was filled right away, and the next thing I knew there were stacks of books under the bed. Then the pile on the table got so big that there was hardly any space for eating and writing.

Once when I was sitting right in the middle of all this mess, my neighbor popped in to borrow a coin to put in the gas meter.

"Why write another book when you already have your room full?" she said as she left.

Have I mentioned that I wasn't the only occupant of my room—that I was sharing it with an owl? If I didn't, I forgot the most important part of the story. When I took over the room from Skipper Jansson, it was on one condition: "You have to take care of my little bird," he said.

"Sure," I said, because I'm very fond of birds. Naturally I thought it was a canary or something like that.

Jansson's directions about how to care for the bird sounded a bit odd, but it never occurred to me that he was talking about an owl!

His name is Smuggler. It didn't take long for us to become friends—that is, once we got to know each other's habits. In the beginning they were quite different. It took me a while to catch on to his eating habits. I thought his diet was a bit monotonous, but I got used to it. And I forgot that Smuggler was an owl, and he forgot that I was a human being. But, to begin with, everything was a bit complicated.

As long as there was daylight Smuggler dozed or slept. He was no problem at all—as a matter of fact,

I hardly knew he was around. But as soon as darkness set in he flew into action and made such a commotion that I hardly got any sleep. Since I couldn't change Smuggler's habits, I obviously had to change mine. I began to do my writing at night while he was flying around. In the beginning it was hard, but gradually I got used to it, and worked by candlelight. Now and then Smuggler would fly over and perch on my typewriter. He would look at me, his eyes glowing in the dark like flickering candles. I've always loved candlelight.

I would probably have been able to manage better if I hadn't had to pile books on my bed, too. I put them under the mattress so that I would have some space to sleep, but the next day I was stiff and sore all over.

Then I tried to sleep sitting on my chair. If Smuggler can sleep sitting up so can I, I said to myself. But it didn't work because I kept toppling over, which of course woke me up.

I was getting pretty tired of the whole setup when one day, falling asleep over the newspaper, my eyes focused on an ad which said: "Sleep while you work." I woke up with a start, feeling a bit guilty. How could they possibly know that I was sitting there sleeping? Then I took a closer look at the ad. It said:

EASY BABYSITTING
Sleep while you work
Work while you sleep
Telephone 123456

I read the words over and over. It sounded too good to be true to be able to sleep while you worked and vice versa—and very practical too. I got up and pulled the telephone out of the bread box. Smuggler has bad habits, or perhaps he doesn't like telephones, but he used it as his private toilet, and I wouldn't put up with that.

I dialed the number and several times got the wrong connection, but when I finally got through I just couldn't stop yawning.

Somebody kept shouting, "Hello, Hello," at the other end of the wire. It must have been the mother of the child, but I was unable to utter a single word.

"Who is it? Hello!"

I tried to stifle the yawn, but it got the better of me. Suddenly there was a silence at the other end of the line, but she hadn't hung up because I heard a yawn, which to my great relief didn't come from me. It came right out of the receiver. Nothing is more contagious than a yawn.

"Excuse me," I said, "but with whom am I yawning?"

"That is what I was just about to ask," she said, laughing.

"Yes, of course," I said. "I'm a bit sleepy. That's why I'm calling—I mean I've just read your ad in the paper and I would very much like to have the job. I think it would suit me perfectly."

"You mean because you're so sleepy?" She was laughing, but I had only myself to blame. I often talk a bit too freely to strangers, especially on the telephone.

After a moment she said: "Don't you have any other qualifications?"

"Qualifications" is a big word you use when you're asking what people can do. What she really meant was: "Can you do anything besides sleep?"

"Have you taken care of children before?"

"Sure," I said, thinking of Smuggler, because he really is like a child.

"This one isn't exactly a baby," she said.

"Nor this one either," I said and bit my tongue. I shouldn't have said that because I don't know how old Smuggler is—I forgot to ask Jansson—and besides, he's an owl and not an infant.

"Do you smoke?" she asked, continuing her cross-examination.

"Oh no, Smuggler wouldn't like that; but when I do it's mint leaves or . . ."

What a fool I was! Why did I have to say that? Of course she immediately wanted to know who Smuggler was. And Smuggler, who can't hear his name mentioned without getting all excited and sounding off, began to fly all around the room. He makes two sounds: "ho-ho-ho" when he is happy and contented, and "tjopp-tjopp" when he is cross. Now he was tjopping, and I just couldn't quiet him down. He didn't understand what I meant, but probably thought that I had talked enough and went on tjopping like mad. That was his way of interrupting the conversation.

"What's that noise?" shouted the mother at the other end of the line.

"It's only my alarm clock . . ."

"What a terrible racket! Can't you shut it off?"

"I'll try."

I made terrible faces at Smuggler, but that only amused him. Luckily he quieted down by himself.

"That's a funny alarm clock," said the mother. "I've never heard anything like it. My daughter has a cuckoo clock. . . ."

"How nice," I said. "May I have the job?"

I had to put an end to the conversation. Smuggler looked impatient, and I was afraid of what he might do.

"One thing more," said the mother. "I would like you to be up and dressed when I come home from work. I'm a nurse and I usually get home about six in the morning. I'm tired then and prefer that you be out of the house—it's hard to be sociable at that hour."

"Sure, I'll be out of the house by six," I said.

Then I remembered Smuggler. He couldn't stay home by himself all night. I would have to bring him along, so I said: "Maybe I had better bring my alarm clock along. Then I'll be sure to wake up."

"Yes, that's a good idea."

"Well then, I'll bring it along. It's very reliable."

I winked at Smuggler so that he would understand that everything was arranged for him, too. But I shouldn't have done that, because he began hopping around me, hooting and flapping his wings. I just had to get this over with!

"When do you want me to come?" I shouted nervously into the receiver.

"Come at two this afternoon so that we can talk. My daughter will be in school. But what on earth is going on? Can you hear me?"

"Yes. Thank you very much. I'll be there."

I hung up and looked around for Smuggler, but he was hiding. He is an expert at disappearing acts.

"Come out you little pest," I hissed at him. "Come out!"

But I had to look for him until I finally found him in my beautiful big copper tea kettle. I use it as a decoration and sometimes I polish it, but not often. That's where Smuggler had decided to hide. I knew it all the time, but of course it wouldn't do to find him right away.

He can't get out of the kettle by himself, so I have to turn it upside down and shake him out. He likes that. He kept on circling around my head; obviously his conscience was bothering him. I got a rag and some polish and began cleaning the kettle. Then he settled down on my head to supervise the job. He knows I like that. He's just about the right weight, and the pressure seems to hold down my thoughts so that they don't fly off in all directions. It may sound funny, but I can think better when Smuggler is sitting on my head, and he's aware of that.

He just perched there without moving, wondering what would happen next. I polished away until the kettle was so shiny that we could see ourselves in it. We looked round and funny and completely different, as though in a crazy mirror, but we recognized each other when our eyes met in the kettle.

"Smuggler," I said, looking into his eyes with my most serious expression, "you and I have to change our habits. We have to start living in the daytime instead of at night."

He said nothing but peered down at me from his perch on my head.

"We might as well start practicing right away," I said. "From now on, no sleeping in the daytime. From now on, we do our sleeping at night."

I took Smuggler down and put him in front of me. He blinked as if he were asking what it was all about. Daylight was streaming into the room. I pulled down the shade, and so changed day into night. The room was suddenly quiet and dark, the way it should be when we have to work.

Smuggler's eyes turned into two burning flames. He began to fly around looking for his food, which I had hidden in flower pots and various other places around the room.

I turned on my working light and began writing about stones—schist, mica, calamine, tourmaline, spinel, lazulite. . . .

JULIA

WHEN MY MOTHER decided that I had to have a night daddy, I was furious. She didn't discuss it with me; she didn't even ask me what I thought of the idea. She just said: "He's coming tonight."

"No, he isn't," I said.

"He most certainly is!"

"I won't let him in. He can ring the bell until he's blue in the face. I won't open the door!"

"He already has the key," she said.

"But I'm big now! I go to school. I can take care of myself. I'm not afraid to be alone." I most certainly did not want a night daddy.

We said the sort of things to each other that people say when they don't agree, but I can't talk about them since they're private. Then we made up, although neither of us gave in.

I thought the whole night-daddy thing was ridiculous, but mommy can be stubborn as a mule when she makes up her mind. You just can't get anywhere with her.

Finally I agreed that he could come *if I didn't have to see him*—which meant after I was in bed. He would not be allowed in my room and had to keep to himself. I didn't want him to bother me. Mommy said I had to behave myself, because the night daddy was very nice, and his feelings might be hurt if I were rude.

I've noticed that grownups can't judge who is nice and who isn't. And they seem to think that people are terribly upset when children are rude. That just isn't so. Either they don't care, or else they get angry and say that you've been badly brought up. Grownups aren't at all as easily hurt as mothers seem to think. They make out all right if one leaves them alone.

"As long as I know that you're not alone here all night long, I don't have to worry," mommy said. I could understand that, so I went along with it for her sake. Otherwise I never would have stood for it.

Before mommy went to the hospital, I made her call the night daddy and tell him not to come before I was in bed, and that he mustn't disturb me. I stood next to her when she talked to him. "O.K." he said at the other end. He seemed to catch on pretty fast from the very beginning.

My mommy isn't married, and I'm just as glad, because then I'd have one of those ordinary fathers and would never have had a night daddy. I never cared for fathers much; they sound very fussy and have to decide everything. My classmates, for instance, always have to ask their fathers' permission, and if they get into trouble, they have to tell their fathers all about it. And "father says this," and "father says that," and they put their noses into everything, and boss everyone around. Doesn't that sound cowardly—to boss those who are smaller than you? And fathers are big and rich and have fancy cars. Everybody is always concerned about how they think and feel, and what they are saying, but you hardly ever get to see them; and if they do show up once in a while, everybody is surprised. They all *look* harmless, just like other old men. They don't talk much—the mothers do most of the talking. But the mothers are always dragging them into the conversation. They're always saying: "That's up to

23

Daddy. Ask Daddy. Daddy said. . . . I'm going to tell your Daddy!" I wouldn't like to have a life like that.

It's just like my teacher and the headmaster, or worse still, like my teacher and God. She keeps talking about him all the time.

Once when she was reading a story about make-believe people, I had the idea that God must be one of them, and I asked her about it. She acted so funny and got all flustered. I still think he is one of her make-believe characters because she doesn't believe in him, not really. I can tell, because when she talks about him she looks the way grownups do when they try to fool children about Santa Claus. She acted as if she thought the whole thing was childish. Mommy doesn't believe in God either, but I do.

I feel sorry for everyone who is nagged at. My night daddy doesn't do that, although I was sure he would and was jumping mad the first few nights. As soon as mommy left, I began thinking about how to greet him. On a piece of paper I printed in big letters:

PRIVATE PROPERTY! DO NOT DISTURB!
TRESPASSING FORBIDDEN!

I taped the note to the outside of my bedroom door. Since I didn't have a key, I had to shove the bureau

in front of the door. Then I put a heavy cowbell on top of the bureau so that it would crash to the floor in case he tried to open the door. Mommy says I sleep like a top; sometimes I only pretend, although she doesn't know that.

Then I went to bed and fell asleep. I didn't even have to pretend. It just happened like that because I had *decided* not to be awake when he came. I know how curious I am by nature, and I didn't want to take any chances that he would see me.

It must have been about midnight when I woke up. It was dark outside, and then I remembered that

I wasn't alone. It must be the night daddy playing a record—a strange kind of music, but I liked it. Then I heard a fluttering noise. What was he doing in there? Sometimes it sounded as if he were saying ho-ho-ho. Very peculiar. He kept on making these mysterious sounds. I just had to get up and see what was going on! But there was that stupid bureau in front of my door. I couldn't even get to the keyhole, so as quietly as I could, I shoved the bureau aside to peek.

I know it isn't very nice to peek through keyholes, but anyway I wasn't able to see a thing. How dumb. I had to open the door just a crack. Luckily he didn't hear me because of the record player.

He was sitting on the floor in front of the fireplace surrounded by lots of big books. He seemed to be far away and didn't see or hear anything. He just kept his nose in those books. He looked ordinary; what I mean is, there was nothing peculiar about him—except that an owl was sitting on his head. It was a live owl, not a stuffed one. Like a flash the owl turned his head toward me and glared. The man sitting on the floor didn't notice a thing. Then the owl began flying around hooting and flapping his wings, and making a terrible racket. Of course the cuckoo would have to strike twelve at that very moment! He flew out of his house and crowed for all he was worth.

What made me do it I don't know, but I grabbed the cowbell and began ringing it. When he looked up I dropped it. There was a terrible crash, but he didn't look a bit surprised, just nodded to me. After that I remember everything we said to each other.

"Hi," he said. "I seem to have forgotten the time. Did the clock strike eleven or twelve?"

"Twelve."

"Goodness, I should have been in bed a long time ago. I had made up my mind to go to bed early, and here I am, still sitting around."

"You can go home and go to bed. I don't need a babysitter," I said.

He was stretching and yawning and looked very sleepy. "I have no intention of being a babysitter," he said. "That's not why I'm here."

"Then why are you here?"

"To have a bed to sleep in."

"Don't you have a bed in your house?"

"Yes, but there is no room for me."

"Is it too small?"

"No, it's full of books. That's why your mother said I could sleep here, since she isn't home. Is that all right with you?"

He looked at me with big eyes that seemed to smile. I liked them from the very beginning.

"I don't mind as long as you don't bother me," I said.

He shook his head and looked very serious. "I'd never dream of doing that," he said. "That is, if you don't bother me. I want to be left in peace."

"So do I."

"O.K. Then we'll each go to our room."

"O.K."

I was about to close the door when I realized that the owl was in my room. He had flown up to the cuckoo clock and was sitting on it hooting in great excitement. Something must have gone wrong because that silly cuckoo just sat there. The owl was somehow keeping it from disappearing back into the clock.

"Look what your owl is doing to my cuckoo clock. You ought to watch your pet," I said.

Without getting the least bit ruffled he called: "Smuggler, come down!" But the owl didn't budge. That was the first time I heard Smuggler's name. It suited him; he looked like a Smuggler somehow.

"Smuggler doesn't seem to want to leave the cuckoo. He wants company."

"But the *cuckoo* doesn't," I said. "He wants to be left alone, just like me."

"You hear that Smuggler! Come down!"

But Smuggler didn't move. He made his tjopping sound and tried to hide behind the cuckoo. It was such a ridiculous sight that it was hard to keep from laughing.

"Smuggler, can't you see that the cuckoo wants to be left alone? Do as I say! Come down!"

Smuggler pretended not to hear. We got nowhere with him and finally had to climb up and get him down, and then the cuckoo immediately disappeared into the clock.

"He'll be back out in an hour," he said to console Smuggler. "Now we'll all go to bed. Good night. Sleep well."

I went into my room and closed the door, but I heard him moving around in there talking to the owl. The owl answered, and it sounded as if they understood each other. I couldn't help listening, although I know it isn't very nice. It sounded so funny —he asked if Smuggler liked me, or if he thought I was too strict. "You probably have to be," he added, "when you suddenly have uninvited guests like you and me to cope with."

He told Smuggler to be gentle with the cuckoo because it was a bit delicate. Although he cuckooed every hour, he didn't have much else to say and it was *I* who was the boss and *I* seemed to decide everything. Of course I do! Then he said that the cuckoo was much better brought up and more obedient than Smuggler.

"The cuckoo only cuckooes when he is supposed to—every hour on the hour. But you, you rascal, you keep on hooting all the time!"

For a while I didn't hear a thing and I began to think they had gone to bed. But after a while there was a knock on my door. It was he.

"Excuse me. Are you asleep?"

"Yes," I said.

"That's too bad."

"Why?"

"It's such a beautiful night."

"What's beautiful?"

"There's a moon and it's raining. . . . I thought you might like to see it. . . ."

That was too much to resist, so I got up and tiptoed over to my window. He was right—it was beautiful. Half of the sky was raining and the other half was glittering with stars. The window was spattered with raindrops that reflected the brightness of the moon. It was a fantastic sight. I didn't say anything; I still didn't know him well enough, even though he no longer bothered me. He was talking to Smuggler again; and maybe I'm imagining things, but his voice sounded a bit disappointed when he said:

"She doesn't answer. Perhaps she's asleep. We mustn't disturb her."

They went to his room and began moving around in there. It took an endless time before they finally settled down. I heard him saying to Smuggler that they had to put in a daylight bulb.

"Look! Isn't this a nice bulb I bought for you? It shines just like the sun." Smuggler sounded very excited.

But a moment later something happened in there. Smuggler began to fly wildly around the room, and I was trying to decide whether or not to go in when I heard him say:

"This is a fine mess! It's pitch black and I don't know my way around the house. . . ."

Then there was a crash followed by a shattering noise. At that point I stormed in.

"What's all this racket?" I cried. "What's going on in here?"

The moon had gone behind a cloud, and the room was indeed so dark that you couldn't see a thing. The only light came from Smuggler's eyes. He was still flying around, hooting like mad. You could tell by the sound that he was enjoying himself immensely.

"What's happened?" I demanded.

"I seem to have blown a fuse. I put in a daylight

bulb for Smuggler because otherwise he can't sleep. Owls are creatures of the night: they sleep during the day and do their living at night. . . ."

"I can see that."

"I just need a light to get him to sleep," he said.

"Wait a minute."

I groped around until I found a candle. "Do you have any matches?" I asked.

He fumbled around and found some. He wanted me to light one, but I couldn't see his hand.

"Light it yourself," I said.

He lit it, and I put the candle down.

"Candlelight makes everything so cozy," he said.

"We have more candles."

"Don't you have any fuses?"

"I like candlelight better."

"Yes, it's much nicer," he agreed. "But Smuggler has to have daylight otherwise he'll never fall asleep."

I tried to remember where mommy kept the fuses, but I didn't have the foggiest idea. Smuggler was wide awake and very lively, so I went to the kitchen and collected all the candles I could find. I found a box of Christmas tree candles and a large assortment of others, which I put in holders and brought in. We lit them one by one, and they gave the room a beautiful glow! But it got warm, and I felt myself getting drowsy.

"Don't you think that Smuggler can sleep now?" I asked.

"Maybe, if he hears his cradle song. . . ."

He put on a record which he had brought along. It was his and Smuggler's lullaby. I hadn't heard it before—no singing, only a dreamy kind of music. Now it's also my lullaby.

For a while Smuggler sat looking at the lights and listening to the music. Then he began blinking his eyes, looking sleepy, and sounding sleepy when he made his little noises.

"It's been a tiring day for him. He's in the process of changing his habits, and that's a hard thing to do," my night daddy said.

"He's actually yawning—did you see?" I asked.

Smuggler liked to perch on a corner of the bed right next to the pillow when he slept. He flew over and settled down there, and after a while tucked his head under his wing.

"He's almost asleep," I whispered. "Good night, Smuggler."

I went back to my room but I left the door open a crack. My night daddy was walking around in there blowing out the candles while listening to the music.

The room became filled with shadows that seemed to move slowly, as if in their sleep. It looked so warm and cozy.

Suddenly he appeared at my door with all the shadows behind him. At first I thought I was dreaming, but then I heard his voice:

"What's your name?"

I was a bit surprised because I thought that mommy had told him.

"Don't you know my name?"

"No."

"Then I won't tell you."

I was pleased at the thought that he would never know my name. Never! I don't like it—it doesn't suit me, and it makes me feel stupid. I've always wanted to change my name.

"I *won't* tell you," I repeated, so he would understand that there was no point in asking any further.

"O.K. But what do you want me to call you?"

"That's up to you."

"Do you want me to think of a name for you?"

He was surprised, of course, but almost as pleased as I was at the idea, and that made me like him.

"What would you like to be called?"

"I don't know—something that would make me feel happy inside."

He came up to my bed, laughing and saying he would have to give it some thought. I realized that, so I kept quiet and didn't disturb him.

After a while he said: "When is your birthday?"

"July seventh."

"July seventh? That's right in the middle of summer when the linden trees are in bloom. Everyone is happy in the summertime—and also at Christmas. Does Christmas make you happy?"

"Sometimes before—but never after."

"O.K. But how about Julia, since you were born in July?"

"Yes, I think so. O.K." I said.

"Good night, Julia."

"Good night."

Then he blew out the candle. I lay there thinking about Julia. It was a lovely name—ever so much prettier than . . . no I won't say it, I'll never say it again.

Then we all went to sleep.

THE NIGHT DADDY

JULIA HAS already filled a lot of pages. Of course I'm curious, but I'm not allowed to look. We've promised not to look at each other's diaries until they are ready. That's the way Julia wanted it. I wondered, how we would know when that would be?

Julia looked at me reproachfully: "I said *ready* not *finished*," she said. "This book must never be finished; that would be too sad. It has to go on and on, but we have to decide when it's ready. We have to, otherwise we'll never get to read what we've written."

I don't want the book to have a definite, final ending either—to come to a full stop, that is. That would almost be like saying good-by. And that just couldn't be. But Julia thinks we'll know when it's ready, so that we can begin reading it. "When the time comes, we'll know it," she says.

I hope so.

We don't have to tell things in the order in which they happened, but in the way we remember them. That's a much more practical way of doing it.

Julia says that she wrote some things down as they were happening. That's the part which especially interests me. Sometimes she used to sit around writing, but I didn't know it was about us—I thought it was homework. What a look Julia gave me when I said that!

She obviously thought I was a square.

"As soon as you pick up a pen, people think you're doing homework," she said in an irritated voice. "How stupid! But if you tell them you've done your homework they don't believe you."

Well, I learned my lesson. You just don't mention school to Julia. That's her private affair. Honestly, I'm relieved that she wants to keep that part of her life to herself, because to talk about school doesn't interest me in the least. It's always bored me. If I have to do it, it's just to be polite. If the situation were reversed, I just wonder how I would feel if some kid started to drill me about my work—just to be polite. I think I'd tell that kid to shut up. But a child wouldn't dare to do that to me. It's really terribly unfair! I wonder how Julia feels about it?

We write on loose-leaf paper, which we then put into a notebook. Julia writes on yellow paper and I on blue so that we don't mix up the notes and read each other's by mistake.

We never write during the day—only at night when we're together. But we never work at the same time. It wouldn't do because then our thoughts might get mixed up.

Julia always writes in her room and then I busy myself with my stones. She likes to write by moonlight, sitting with her feet on the window sill. She takes off her shoes and stockings, wiggles her toes, and writes away furiously. She has her mind set on what she is doing and tells me I ought to do the same.

It's sometimes very hard for me to get started. I feel as if I have a lot to say, but something gets in the way—I don't know what. Just now, for instance, something seems to be stopping me.

"You ought to bathe your feet in the moonlight. You have no idea how good it feels," says Julia dreamily.

"Maybe I ought to try."

Julia has just gone to bed. The moon is still bright.

Maybe I should follow her suggestion. I do hope that no one is watching! I'm hiding behind the curtain and only my feet are sticking out. They look as if they belonged to a ghost: the moon is shining right through them. The moon bath feels good!

Tonight I feel like retelling a short story I once read somewhere—one I told to Julia one night when I was in the same nonworking mood as tonight and couldn't write about stones. In fact I was feeling so lazy that I couldn't even write about us—me, Julia, and Smuggler. I'm reminded of the story when I see my feet reaching toward the moon and shining brightly like a crystal chandelier. These feet don't seem to be part of me right now. How lucky they are to be free from me for a while! I'm feeling very solemn, but also giddy and ready to burst out laughing as I bend forward and blow on my toes. They seem to flicker like candles. . . .

My story is very short. I'm not sure I remember it correctly, but I'll write it down anyway—mostly because of the question Julia will ask afterward—if she gets the point.

Once upon a time there was a toad. He was jumping around in the moonlight. He was thirsty—or perhaps he wanted to bathe his feet—not in moonlight but in water. Or maybe he only wanted to see his reflection in a puddle—I have no way of knowing.

I'm very fond of toads. They have a special way of moving around, and they have beautiful eyes, but that's about all I know about them.

Well, as I was saying, the toad was moving along in its toadlike way toward the puddle. But there wasn't much water in it, and he gazed at it with his sad, beautiful eyes.

"Dry again?" said the toad to the puddle.

"How could I be anything else?" sighed the puddle and shrank still more, so that all that was left of him was a tiny wet spot. "How can I be anything

41

else when I have to give the sea a drink? And the sea is always thirsty!"

That's all there is to the story. After I had told my story, Julia looked at me with her big, dark eyes.

"Am I the toad?" she asked.

I didn't know what to answer, but I think I shook my head and said I didn't know.

But now I do. No, Julia, I'm the toad. It's a bit hard to figure out, because I'm both the toad who wants to drink—or perhaps bathe and look at his reflection—and the puddle that waits for the rain. And I'm also the sea that is always thirsty.

Anyway, that's how I feel sometimes when I want to write and can't. You see now why I sometimes have problems, and that you have to be patient with me.

But if you wanted to be the rain, Julia—the rain that fills the puddle so that the toad could see his reflection and the sea could get a drink of water—it would make me very happy.

JULIA

I AM WRITING this while it is actually happening—
on the second night when he is supposed to come
and I am lying here waiting. This is messy because
I'm writing in bed. But he says it doesn't show when
it's printed. That's a shame though, because no one
will see my pale-yellow writing paper—the color of
the moon and Smuggler's eyes.

How stupid—how awfully stupid—of me to tell
him that I didn't want to be disturbed, although of
course I had no way of knowing what he would be
like. But why did I have to say that he couldn't come
before I was in bed? That's what mommy told him
because that's what I had said.

And then there was that stupid sign I put outside my door! Why did I have to go and do that? "DO NOT DISTURB!" If I erase the DO NOT it will be O.K. Now it reads: "PRIVATE PROPERTY! DIS-TURB! FORBIDDEN!" Should I also erase "FOR-BIDDEN"? No. I'll let that stand. Otherwise it wouldn't be a real sign.

But why doesn't he come?

It's a good thing that I haven't brushed my teeth because he might want some milk and buns. He might not want to eat alone, although mommy says he eats before he leaves home. But he might get hungry on the way, and those buns are delicious!

Goodness, how sticky and crumbly my bed is!

It's strange how many sounds you hear when you're waiting for someone—sounds that you wouldn't otherwise hear. There are buzzing, flush-ing, and clicking sounds. Doors open and close, and there is constant talking and moving around, and then you think—now! But it's always a false alarm! You soon find out that those are only the *waiting* sounds. When you begin to wait, you listen to every sound until you finally put your hands to your ears, because you get so sick and tired of being fooled every single time!

Suppose he doesn't like those buns! Maybe he

would like some other snack instead—maybe some herring. But fish—ugh! what an awful thought! It even smells on paper! But I can't stand this waiting much longer.

Someone is coming up the stairs. They're here! They aren't exactly being quiet, because Smuggler is hooting so that it echoes through the whole house.

I'm going to make believe I'm asleep, and then they'll have to wake me.

It didn't work out exactly as I had planned. I pretended so well that they actually believed me! He opened the door very carefully and hushed Smuggler so that he wouldn't disturb me, and for once that stupid Smuggler obeyed!

They peered at me through the crack in the door, and then he closed it again. And here I am! I'm trying to snore as loud as I can so that he'll come back and give me a shove. Children can damage their nasal passages by snoring that hard! You might even get some kind of infection from it—or doesn't he know about that? It could be dangerous. . . .

I hear them settling down in there. Now he is taking some logs out of the copper bin and making a fire, and now he is putting on that record again. . . .

He said that I was sound asleep and mustn't be

disturbed because I had to get up for school in the morning. But didn't he see the sign that said, "DISTURB!"?

"But, Smuggler, you and I don't have to think about school. We can sit around in our owl fashion for a while longer," he said. Then Smuggler began to sound off because he had heard the word "owl," and the night daddy had to explain that all he meant by "sitting around in owl fashion" was not going to bed. Smuggler is very wise, and he seemed to understand that.

But why don't they wake me up! It's no fun just lying here. By now he is probably buried in his books. . . .

How stupid I am! If I could pretend to be asleep, I can also pretend that they woke me up. That's what

I'll do! If I stay in bed I'll only keep on thinking about that television program. Why did I have to watch that?

I'll say that they woke me up when they came in and Smuggler started to hoot, and that I'd forgotten to brush my teeth, and that there are buns in the kitchen. That's what I'll tell them!

THE NIGHT DADDY

I DON'T KNOW WHY, but I expected Julia to be waiting up for us when we came. I was a bit disappointed not to see her. I thought we had become friends, and I had been looking forward to seeing her again. This was our second night, and Smuggler and I were very glad to be there. I remember running up the stairs two at a time. Julia lives on the top floor of an old apartment house. I whistled and Smuggler hooted so that she would know we were there.

But there wasn't a sound. At first I thought she was playing a game with us, so I went to her door and opened it just a crack, and there she was in her bed, snoring away. I knew that she was only pretending, so I expected her to burst out laughing any minute. I waited, but apparently she had decided not to wake up.

So Smuggler and I were left to amuse ourselves. We're used to that and we didn't mind. We went into the living room, made ourselves at home, and I started to work.

Suddenly Julia appeared in the doorway looking a bit miffed.

"You woke me up," she said.

"I'm sorry, I didn't mean to. I just wanted to see whether you were there. The apartment was so quiet. . . ."

"I was sleeping!"

"Yes, I saw that you were in a deep and *loud* sleep!"

She looked at me suspiciously, as if trying to decide whether I had caught on. But I assumed a look of childish innocence (are children all that innocent —*are* they, Julia?).

After she had glowered at me for a while, she became a bit friendlier.

"I don't mind that you woke me up," she said, "because I had forgotten to brush my teeth."

Then she went over to Smuggler and said hello to him, but he was a bit drowsy from the fire or else he had adapted to the new schedule of sleeping at night. He looked very sleepy and was perched on the bed with his head sunk into his body. He looked just like a ball, but his eyes kept on blinking.

"Are you mad at me, Smuggler?" Julia asked.

"Not at all," I broke in. "He's just sleepy, the way you were a while ago."

"Maybe he's only pretending," she said.

"Oh no!" I said. "Whatever gave you that idea?"

She gave me a quick look, and I gave her an innocent smile in return.

"How can you know how Smuggler feels?" she said.

"I do, because we know each other quite well."

Julia didn't answer. She looked very serious and I wished that I could read her thoughts. Then she said:

"But you're not an owl. How can you be so sure that you understand Smuggler? Although both mommy and I are human beings, we sometimes don't understand each other at all."

I didn't have an answer to that one. I hadn't ever really given much thought to the difference between an owl and a human being. It was so obvious that it had never even occurred to me! But Julia's remark gave me a bad conscience. She looked at me with a thoughtful and wistful expression and then said in a low voice:

"Are you the only one Smuggler has in the world?"

"Yes. Do you feel sorry for him?"

"I don't know. Have you known each other for a long, long time?"

"A long time, yes, but not always. He used to live with a sea captain called Jansson. When Jansson had to move, he left Smuggler with me."

"Hasn't he ever met another owl?"

"Not that I know of—that is, not while I've been taking care of him. He was only a baby when Jansson found him. He'd fallen out of his nest."

"Did he have any sisters or brothers?"

"Probably. Why?"

Julia took her time in answering, and avoided my eyes.

"Oh nothing. But now I'm going to brush my teeth. Good night."

Then off she went, leaving me with Smuggler, who was still sitting in the same spot. I suddenly felt so terribly sorry for him that I choked up. I had the feeling that he was giving me a reproachful look, and that made me very unhappy. Was I ruining someone's life?

I went up to Smuggler and looked him straight in the eyes. "Am I ruining your owl's life, Smuggler?"

Then he flew up and settled himself on my head.

"Can you forgive me for not being an owl, Smuggler?" I whispered.

He seemed to feel that he could, because by way of an answer he hooted.

"We've had a fine time together you and I—or do you sometimes wish you could be with other owls?"

It didn't sound as if he were unhappy—at least not at the moment. He seemed quite content so I relaxed, opened my book, and read out loud to collect my thoughts.

Then Julia was back standing in the doorway. "Are you reading again?"

"Mmmm. . . ."

"Do you *have* to read all the time?"

"Yes."

"Why?"

"Because of the book I'm writing. . . ."

That was the first time I had mentioned to Julia that I was going to write a book. She gave me a disapproving look, or perhaps it was an impatient one, I don't know.

"If you're going to write a book, you ought to *write* and not read."

She sounded angry and annoyed, and I didn't think there was any point in discussing the matter further, so I asked if she had brushed her teeth.

"There's no hurry. . . ."

"But aren't you going to school tomorrow?"

"I suppose I have to. What kind of book are you writing?"

"It's about stones. But look here! If you have to get up early tomorrow morning, wouldn't it be better . . . ?"

She knew what I was about to say and interrupted me: "Are you hungry? I am!"

I had eaten before I left home, so I wasn't very hungry—and not very quick on the trigger either—so I said: "I can make you a sandwich if you want me to."

"We have delicious buns in the kitchen," she said by way of reply.

As I said, I was a bit slow; besides I wanted to work. "Do you want me to get you a bun?" I asked her.

She sounded disappointed.

"I can get it myself. Good night Stone Daddy."

She closed the door with a bang. I stood there looking stupid, and feeling stupid too. I didn't know what to do, so I put on a record and tried to read.

"What's that you're playing?"

There was Julia again! I had just settled down and was beginning to concentrate.

"What did you say?"

"About that sandwich you promised me—I want it now."

"You'll have to eat it in bed—and promise to go to sleep afterward!"

"I want cheese on rye."

"O.K."

I went to the kitchen and made her a delicious sandwich, which I put on a plate and brought in to her. She was sitting up in bed writing. She looked at the sandwich. "All the cheese is in the middle," she said. "There is hardly any on the edges."

"It's a very good sandwich," I said in a voice that was just about to explode.

"Yes," she said.

"And then you'll sleep like a log!"

"Mmmmm. . . ."

"Good night."

"Good night. It's all right that there wasn't enough cheese around the edges."

"O.K. Sleep tight."

I went out and shut the door to make it absolutely clear that this was the end. It was night, and night was for sleeping. I poked around in the fireplace and added a couple of logs. Then I settled down to some reading at last.

But the book had disappeared! I thought I might have taken it out to the kitchen, but it wasn't there. I hunted all over until I finally found it under the pillow I was sitting on! I have no idea who put it there, but of course it could have been me! Naturally I had lost my place on top of it all! I've never learned to use a bookmark, and I sighed as I kept turning the pages. I felt my temper rising, and then I heard a small voice, by this time very familiar:

"I can't sleep."

"Haven't we met before?" I snarled, throwing the book on the floor. *What is it this time?*"

"My bed is full of crumbs."

"Why don't you brush them away?"

"Because. . . ."

We went to her room, and I brushed and shook as I've never brushed and shaken anything in all my life. When I was through there wasn't a single crumb left in the bed.

"So now you're going to sleep *like a top* until tomorrow morning!"

"You may have this bookmark."

It was a very pretty bookmark—a cat with a pink, glittery ball of yarn. "A bookmark is exactly what I need," I said.

"I realized that," said Julia.

I had pangs of conscience because I had suspected her of hiding the book when it was I who had misplaced it. I bent down and tucked her in.

"Do black people become white when they become angels?" she asked.

I had never thought about that.

"Why should they?" I said.

"Ulla and the rest of the kids say that all angels are white."

"How do they know?"

"Then why aren't there any bookmarks with black angels? I've always wanted a collection of black angels."

"They must have black-angel bookmarks in Africa."

Julia was thinking this over. I could tell because she was frowning.

"If black people have black angels, do they also have black ghosts?"

"Maybe—that is, if they believe in ghosts."

"Well, then they would have to spook in the middle of the day, because at night they couldn't be seen since they're black."

This set off an interesting chain of thought that was new to me, but Julia had to go to bed and I had work to do. I tried to end the conversation, but she wouldn't let me go.

"Guess what I did today?" she said.

I shook my head.

"I watched television, but don't tell mommy because I'm not allowed to watch when I'm alone."

"What did you watch?"

She hesitated before answering, so I was quite surprised when she shrugged her shoulders and said:

"Nothing special. I've almost forgotten it."

"Oh."

"I think it was about a black funeral," she added.

I told her I had also seen that funeral on television. Julia gave me a penetrating look.

"Have you also almost forgotten it?"

"No," I said, because I hadn't.

"Then you must be feeling sad."

It took me a while before I could answer that one —not because I was really sad, but because all of a sudden I didn't feel like saying good-night to Julia. I didn't want to leave her just then.

"No, I'm not sad," I said. "But I'm hungry. How about . . . ?"

I've never seen anyone so happy about someone else's hunger. Julia leaped out of bed.

"I'm starving!" she said. "We have the most delicious buns in the kitchen. Let's put the lights on so that Smuggler can sleep."

But we found him already sound asleep in the living room. The warmth of the fire had had its effect on him.

We decided to have our little party on the balcony. The view is sensational from Julia's apartment. It overlooks the rooftops, and in the distance, the church. The church steeple has a clock that strikes every fifteen minutes. When you're on the balcony, it sounds as though it were striking right over your head.

We set the table in a festive way, with a flowered tablecloth, tall glasses, the basket with the buns, and a lantern as a centerpiece.

It was very gay. Julia ate an incredible amount of

buns, and so did I; but neither of us got a stomach-ache afterward.

Then I smoked my pipe, and we played some records. It was late—much too late for Julia.

"Do you think you'll be able to sleep better now?" I asked Julia as I tucked her in.

"Yes, I'm sure I will," she said.

A while later as I was lying in bed trying to decide what to read, I heard Julia's door creak as she slowly opened it. I made a mental note to put some oil in the hinges, and then looked up. Julia was standing there in her white nightgown, her hand on the doorknob.

"Are you asleep?" she whispered.

"Yes, as you can see," I said.

"We forgot the bedtime story. . . ."

She tried to arouse my interest by playing it cool. I didn't say a word—but just stared at her.

"But don't bother to get up because I'm going to tell you one," she said.

She let go of the doorknob and came up to me.

"May I sit on your bed?"

"Yes. But don't wake Smuggler. You have to whisper."

She nodded, and her eyes had that dark sparkle.

"I made it up just now. . . ."

"That sounds exciting. Do tell it."

She settled at the foot of my bed and tucked her nightgown under her knees.

"Are you cold?"

She shook her head, hooked her two big toes together, folded her hands under her chin, and began:

(I've asked Julia to write down the story in her own words because it would be much better than my repeating it. At first she refused, but then she gave in.)

"Once there was a Negro king who became dead. But of course he was only pretending, so that all the bad people in the world would be sad, but they weren't, because they were *that* stupid! But he fooled them because when they were going to bury him, he hid in the flowers on top of the casket, making himself look like a cross. There were great windows behind him that sparkled, although everything else was dark. When they began singing in the church, something very strange happened. The flowers on the coffin flew out of the windows, and all of a sudden everything was bright, and the Negro king lay hidden among the flowers. Then he flew out, too, and they kept on singing, louder and louder. And he flew out to all the people who were waiting for him outside. They said he wasn't dead at all—only stupid people believed that because they didn't understand. And that's the end of the story."

JULIA

IF YOU WALK in the rain when the stones are wet, as we did, you see that my night daddy is right; they aren't gray at all! They have a lot of color if you look at them closely.

I've looked in his stone books and seen pictures of stones so beautiful that you think you're dreaming. It's hardly possible to believe that they're real.

Just think—billions and millions of years ago people didn't exist, but there were these tiny, tiny animals, so small that no one could see them.

They probably couldn't even see each other because they were so small. They were beautiful, and they had shells that glowed. But with time they turned into stone—that was their fate; that's what had to happen to them. I've seen a stone like that—my night daddy has one. Millions and billions of tiny animals can fit into it, but you can't see them because they've turned into colors, and that's what you see.

Stones are real secrets, and now I know why he has to write about them. I didn't understand what it was all about before.

But there is another reason why he wants to write about them. Something happened when he was a child that had to do with a stone. When he told me about it, I remembered something that happened when I was little that also had to do with a stone. I thought I had forgotten all about it, but when he asked me to tell him what happened, I remembered everything.

We were talking about what had happened to us a long time ago, although of course we didn't know each other then, and lived far away from each other. Maybe I didn't even exist when he had his experience with the stone.

That was when I knew that I didn't want any other daddy for the rest of my life. A night daddy is a real daddy; you can tell him just about everything because he knows what you mean and understands you.

I'll tell my story first because it's short, and then he can tell his afterward.

When I was little I didn't know that you had to have money when you wanted to buy something. I thought that if you had a thing you really treasured, you could go to a store and get something for it in return. That's how I thought things worked.

One day I found a green stone in the gutter. At first I thought it was a marble that had split in two, but when I picked it up I saw that it wasn't half a marble because it was green all the way through. It was a real stone, shiny and smooth all the way around, and wonderful to touch. I know you shouldn't put stones and things you find in your mouth, but this was a very *special* stone. I just *had* to put this one in my mouth! It had such a shiny taste. When I ran around a lot and got thirsty, I would put the stone in my mouth and stand absolutely still, and then I wasn't thirsty any more. That was in the summer. But winter came, and then you don't get so thirsty. In winter, though, I get such a terrible craving for candy that I can hardly think about anything else. One day when there was a snowstorm and the wind was howling, and I was feeling very lonely because Ulla and her crowd wouldn't speak to me, I ran down to the candy store with the stone, almost without knowing what I was doing. An old man was standing there, leaning over the counter looking at all the goodies. He was carrying a cane. I didn't realize that he was next but walked up, put my stone on the counter, and just stood there waiting.

When I was little I thought that everyone could read my thoughts so I didn't say anything. I just stood around, expecting people to give me what I wanted. The girl behind the counter picked up the stone. "Are you giving it to me?" she asked.

I nodded. She took the stone, and when I didn't budge she looked surprised.

"Did you want to use it to buy something?" she asked.

I pointed to some raspberry candy and some caramels, which I thought would be the least she would give me in exchange. But all she did was laugh and put the stone back on the counter.

"Don't you know that you can't buy things with stones?" she said and laughed so hard I felt my cheeks getting red. I quickly hid my stone and felt ashamed, and sorry for the stone, too.

The old man still stood there, unable to make up his mind, but he looked at me, poked me with his stick, and asked if he could have a look at the stone. He put on his glasses and looked at it for a long time, turned it around and examined it closely and from far away, and then he said:

"And to think that a thing of beauty doesn't even fetch a caramel."

I remember his exact words, although I didn't understand what they meant until later. I always remember words, even if they don't register at the time. They sounded so funny in the midst of all the goodies—and the stone floor and the display case gave the words a strange echo. Behind the counter was a mirror in which I could see everything—myself, and the old man holding the stone, and the girl behind the counter who kept on laughing. I couldn't understand what was so funny. I turned and bolted out of there. I didn't remember the stone until I got home. Then I ran all the way back, but the old man had already left. I didn't go inside, but looked through the window and didn't see him. I never got the stone back, and I never saw the old man again. He was so old he probably died.

"What makes you think he died?" asked my night daddy when I said that.

I didn't know why, but he was old, although that wasn't the reason. I said it without thinking—not knowing what I really meant. I think I said it because it sounded *nasty*. Sometimes when I've had a mean thought, I say something like that (I don't really think it!) so that the mean feeling won't come back.

I didn't answer his question, and that's why I'm

writing it now, so that he can read it himself and tell me if he knows some better way to get rid of mean feelings, when you're not sad or angry, but just feeling *nasty*.

Now it's his turn to tell his stone story, and I'm sure it's much longer than mine.

THE NIGHT DADDY

THIS HAPPENED during a summer I spent on the seashore a long time ago. My father and I were walking along the beach. It was very windy, and our voices were practically ripped out of our throats, so that we were hardly able to talk. My father wore a blue beach robe that flapped in the wind. Suddenly he stopped, picked up something from the beach, and handed it to me.

It was a pitch-black stone, quite large. It had been polished by the sea so that it was perfectly smooth. But the odd thing about it was that it had the shape of a heart. But you could tell that it was the sea, and not the human hand, that had formed it.

Then autumn came and school started.

I carried that black stone with me all the time. I always held it in my left hand—it seemed to fit perfectly there. I wasn't nearly so comfortable with it in my right hand. I was convinced that the sea had worked on that stone for thousands and thousands of years to make it fit perfectly into the palm of my left hand. That made it magic, and I couldn't live without it.

I had a friend whose name was Arne. He was my best friend, but sometimes he went around with a boy called Gunnar, who wasn't my friend at all. I could never depend on Arne, but we had fun just the same.

Every day when we left school, we passed by a small, dingy store with an old-fashioned vending machine outside. Arne and I rarely had money in our pockets, but we always stopped to look at it, because it was so creaky and funny.

It was an old wooden thing, reddish-brown, grimy and dirty, and the glass was all scratched. It was almost impossible to see what was inside those compartments. When you inserted a coin, the machine groaned and moaned, and you couldn't choose what you wanted but had to take pot luck.

"It's just as well that we don't have any money

since you can't choose what you want," Arne said. But I don't think he really meant that.

One afternoon we discovered that there was a crack in the lowest shelf of the box, and on that shelf was a big chocolate bar. A small hand could get in and pull it out. My hand just made it, but the sharp edge cut into my wrist, and for a moment I thought I was stuck. The chocolate bar broke in half, but I didn't let go. I was shaking all over, but finally I got it out, with Arne's eyes glued on me.

The chocolate was wrapped in white foil with *CREME DE VANILLE* printed in gold letters. It was a bitter chocolate filled with a white, yummy vanilla cream, and had the most sensational smell. Feeling nervous and guilty, we shared the spoils, telling ourselves and each other that we would never do it again.

The next day when we sneaked up to look at the empty compartment in the vending machine, lo and behold! There was a brand new chocolate bar, exactly like the other one. It was Sunday, and we thought it might be a trap to catch the thief. We kept pacing up and down in front of the machine, looking in every direction. But there was a Sunday emptiness about the place, and there wasn't a soul around. We looked at each other; the same thought struck us both at the same moment. Wasn't it only fair that we share the guilt? Shouldn't Arne also get into the act just to even the score?

Yes, that's the way it had to be. But Arne's hand couldn't get through the opening. There were a few awful moments before he was able to wrench himself loose. And that only made me feel twice as guilty. Arne said that it was his turn to be guilty this time, but that didn't make things any easier for me. It was my hand that took out the chocolate bar. I could have refused, but it was already broken, and we didn't think there was any point in leaving it. Again we shared the stolen goods, sneaked off, and felt rotten through and through. There seemed no way of turning back and going straight any more.

Every day there was in the same place a new chocolate bar which caught our eye as we walked by. We backed away in terror each time we saw it, but at the same time we were irresistibly drawn to it. There was something magic, something supernatural about the whole thing.

We were sure by now that we were in the claws of the devil. The chocolate bars were put there to tempt us, and we fell into the trap each time. We had really become hardened criminals!

In school we just happened to be reading about how criminals were punished in ancient times. A thief got his hand chopped off—the hand that had committed the crime.

Suddenly I felt a sharp pain in my wrist just where the edge of the machine had cut.

During our recreation period Arne said: "What did they do with a *leftie*? They couldn't very well chop off his *right* hand, could they? They would have to ask before they chopped it off."

I'm a leftie but Arne isn't. So I said to him, feeling a bit pleased with myself:

"But they would have no problem deciding what to do with you since you're right-handed."

"But since I couldn't even get my hand in . . ."

There was no doubt as to who was the guilty one. His only contribution was to help me eat the chocolate.

We came to the point where we realized that this had to stop. This was absolutely the last time that we would pilfer the vending machine. Just because there happened to be a new chocolate bar every day didn't necessarily mean that we *had* to take it. But somehow we couldn't just stop like that. We had to plan a proper ending to the life of crime we had gotten ourselves into.

We decided to take our last chocolate bar and use it as an *offering*. By this time we were very fond of the vanilla cream that oozed out of the chocolate, and we couldn't think of a better way of atoning for our sins than to sacrifice it.

So when we had managed to get a bar out once more, we put it into a cigar box and solemnly marched up to the highest hill in town. There we dug a hole, lined it with stones, and put our box in it.

Then for our ceremony we pricked our index fingers with a pin, and each squeezed out some blood, which we mixed. With it we wrote on a piece of paper: "TO THE UNKNOWN." Neither of us dared ask God directly for forgiveness. Maybe he didn't even have anything to do with it; it wasn't his chocolate bar after all. So we decided "not to take the name of the Lord in vain." To the victor belonged the spoils, that is, the chocolate bar.

The unknown—it could have been God himself, of course, but it could also have been the unknown owner of the vending machine. . . .

We put the paper with the text written in blood into the box and buried it. Then it struck us both that this wasn't the right way to do it after all. In order to know how really hard this sacrifice was, we should at least have had a taste. So we dug up the box, each of us had a bite of candy, and then reburied it. The sacrifice was completed.

But that night I had an uneasy feeling. I just had

to go back to the burial place and make sure that nothing had happened to our offering.

When I dug up the box I saw to my astonishment that it was empty. The paper with our blood-writing and the wrapping were all that was left.

What was the explanation? When I told Arne what had happened, he said he already knew all about it. He had been there before me and also discovered that the box was empty. He looked very shaken. According to him, it was the Unknown who had accepted the sacrifice and immediately devoured it to make sure he wouldn't be cheated out of it.

The whole thing was spooky and I didn't feel as liberated and cleansed of the crime as I had hoped.

At a religious-education lecture, the teacher twice repeated something that seemed aimed directly at me: "When you give something away it must be meaningful, not just something that you happen not to need."

I felt myself breaking out into a sweat. I was a spoiled, selfish creature who only gave away the things I didn't need. In my whole life I had never given anything away that I would have wanted myself.

I went straight home from school and gathered together all the books and magazines I really cared about. It turned out to be an enormous pile, which I gave to a drive to help needy children in Norrland.

Then I sat down on a park bench to try to find out whether I *felt* the loss. It didn't take me too long to see through myself. I'd already read the books I was giving away! Again I was parting with things I didn't need!

I couldn't hide the truth from myself any longer. The one thing that would hit me hard would be to give away the stone which my father had given me. It was a terrible decision to have to make, but I just had to do it. I had to give away that black stone heart.

But to whom? My first impulse of course was to give it to Arne. Yet then it would still belong to me in a way, and Arne might feel that he wanted to be my close friend for good. He might even drop Gunnar. I would gain something by giving it to Arne. But that would defeat the purpose of the whole thing. I just couldn't give it to him!

After a night of soul-searching, I knew that there was only one person to whom I could give that stone, so that I would really *feel* it, and that was Ejvor. She was the dumbest, ugliest girl in school. Everyone just seemed to sink into the ground when she approached. When it was convenient she could be quite nice, but then she would turn around and say nasty things behind your back.

The next day when I saw Ejvor, I didn't run the way I used to; instead I walked her part of the way home.

When we came to a corner, I stopped and gave her the stone.

"It's yours," I said, and ran.

I felt her staring at me, and I turned around and caught a glimpse of her eyes, wide with surprise and suspicion.

After that I avoided her more than ever. After all I had earned that right; I had given her my most precious possession.

But once when I ran into her I couldn't keep myself from asking about the stone, which I had never forgotten.

"Oh that silly old stone, I think I must have lost it!" she said. "*Lost it.*" Those were her words!

I noticed that Julia was all ears as I was telling my stone story. She didn't interrupt a single time, and for Julia that's most unusual. When I had finished, her eyes were darker than ever. She sat there without moving or saying a word, just staring into space.

Suddenly she shook her head and whispered:

"No, she didn't lose it. It was the Unknown. He knew that it was an offering to him, and he made sure that he got it. Don't think for a minute that he would let that Ejvor keep it. That's marvelous because now you know that he has the stone. Now we know for sure where it is!"

That hadn't occurred to me. Of course she was right! I was so relieved when Julia came up with the answer because I've always regretted giving away that stone! My father had given it to me, and I had given it away for such a stupid reason—no reason at all. But then it hadn't been in vain. . . .

Julia is wise; she knows the answer to a lot of things.

JULIA

Now I HAVE TO SAY something about Ulla and her crowd, although I wish I didn't have to, because they're all so stupid. A long time ago, in first grade, Ulla was really a pal of mine. She gave me an alarm clock she had found. It was broken, but only the clapper was missing, so I stuck a piece of wire into the hole and attached a pearl to it. It worked and gave off such a nice sound! I still have it.

When I showed it to Ulla after I had repaired it, there was a kind of funny look on her face.

"Look! The clock has gotten its voice back," I said. "There is a little tongue making noises inside."

The pearl I fixed it with is red, just like a tongue.

But she hardly looked at it. Birgit was with her, and they both giggled.

"What a silly thing to do," they said.

I thought she'd be pleased that I'd been able to fix the clock she gave me, but she wasn't at all.

That's because she has *three* best friends and I have only *one*. Kerstin comes first, then Birgit, and I'm the third. I'm only asked to play with her when Kerstin and Birgit are busy. All they seem to do is fool around and say silly things—and brag and tell fibs and fight—and tattle to the teacher about me, and say that *I* fight and tell lies. They say it's because I haven't been brought up properly and because I don't have a father; and that's what their mothers say, too. They also say that they pity me, but I don't think they ought to. Once I told them a lie—that was a long time ago when I was in the first grade. I told them that of course I had a father, but he was away most of the time.

"Prove it!" yelled Birgit.

Then I showed them a picture of my uncle, and that shut them up. But once when Ulla was at our house, she saw the picture and asked my mother: "Is this her father?"

Mommy told her the truth, that it was my uncle, and then Ulla told everyone in school and said that I had lied. The teacher also heard about it; and with the same expression she used at morning chapel, she said that I must really be longing for a real father since I had told such a big lie, and that therefore everything was forgiven. I retorted that it wasn't the reason, and the lie wasn't forgiven because it was so stupid. When I said that, all they did was laugh. It seems that it's worse to confess to a lie than to tell one because Ulla said:

"You're not going to be my third best friend any more. Anne will."

But then she and Anne had a falling out about trading pictures of movie stars, and she took me back. I had to promise to make myself scarce when Kerstin and Birgit came around, "because you know you're only the next, next best," said Ulla.

I don't need to be told that.

But she's still my best friend, and when we're alone she is very nice to me. I forget that I'm only her third best friend, and I think she forgets it too, because we have such a good time together. We walk along streams in the woods and just pretend. Ulla has a lot of imagination, but if one of her friends shows up, she gets very uppity and says she's glad they came so that she doesn't have to play games any more. Then she holds her nose and says I have to go home to my mother and have my diapers changed; and she doubles over, pretending to be sick while she is really just laughing.

One day when Ulla and I were building a hut with some old crates we had gotten from the grocer, the girls turned up. We were having such fun hammering and doing the work all by ourselves. She said that it was to be our secret, but when they turned up she forgot all about that. They told me to get lost, and they bombarded me with burrs, which got stuck in my hair so mommy had to cut it and I looked awful afterward. That's the way it always ends.

Ulla and I walk to and from school together because we live near each other, and every afternoon when we part she says: "See you tomorrow, twenty of eight in front of Jonsson's. But she is never on time, and I stand there waiting until she appears like a small dot at the end of the street. Seeing me doesn't make her move any faster. I've tried to come later, to make *her* wait and see how it feels, but that didn't work. She doesn't wait—she just takes off.

"After all, you know you're only my third best friend," she says. "Birgit and Kerstin would be mad if I waited for you."

I'm sick and tired of the whole business. Ulla isn't going to be my best friend any more, because when

I told her about my night daddy, she said that I was lying. "There's no such thing," she said. "Either you have a father or you don't."

"Of course there are such things as stepfathers," Kerstin said, "but I wouldn't want one of them. Is your mother going to get married?"

"No," I said.

"Then she's lying," Birgit said to Kerstin, and they looked through me as if I didn't exist any more.

"But I can prove it," I screamed.

Then Ulla turned toward me with a sneer: "Don't tell me you're going to produce another old uncle!" Then they went into a fit of giggles. But it doesn't take much to set them off.

I just don't know what I'd do without my night daddy. I wouldn't be able to stand Ulla and the others if I didn't have him. I can't even stand writing about it. Luckily I forget fast. I can't help remembering some of it, but the worst part I always forget.

I'm going to write about something nicer: my night daddy.

Yesterday he was rather odd. Usually he has his nose in the same book. Stones seem to be hard going, and he seldom turns a page. But yesterday everything was different; he sat there furiously thumbing through the book. Then he tossed it aside and

picked up another one. He kept on scratching his head and puffing on his pipe until he had a coughing fit. And then when Smuggler wanted to be friendly and sit on his head, he shooed him away, although he has always said that he could think better when Smuggler sat on his head.

He wasn't angry—he just looked absentminded.

Something was wrong, although I didn't want to ask. I understand, because when people ask me what's wrong, I always answer "nothing!" You have to decide for yourself whether you want to talk about it or not. I decided to wait it out, but he was still stony silent, so I began talking to Smuggler instead.

Of course that made Smuggler hoot, so I had to work at quieting him down.

"Smuggler, don't make so much noise. Don't you see that he's got something on his mind? Something is bothering him, making him sad." Suddenly he stopped thumbing through his book.

"What did you say? Who's sad?"

"I was only talking to Smuggler," I said.

"Smuggler doesn't seem to be worried about anything," he said. Since he didn't seem to understand what I meant, I added:

"We were talking about you."

"About me? Is there anything wrong with me?"

"Yes, there is."

"Well, I hadn't realized that. Maybe I just got out of bed on the wrong side this morning."

That's one of those stupid remarks grownups make when they don't want to tell the truth, and that wasn't like him.

"Is that what your mother used to say to you?" I asked.

"Yes," he said and laughed. "How did you know?"

"Because my mother always says the same thing. But I know I always get out of my bed on the same side."

"Come to think of it, I do, too," he said with a sigh, and began thumbing through his book again.

"You're in a very funny mood today," I said. By now I had decided to find out what the trouble was.

Then he confided in me. He said he just couldn't work. He said he couldn't write a word. That's hard to understand, because once you've learned how to write, it's just as easy as talking.

But maybe it was because I was bothering him; he probably wanted to be alone.

"I'll go to bed if you like," I said, "although mommy said that I could stay up later tonight."

"Of course you can. It's Sunday tomorrow and you're not bothering me."

"But there's something wrong, isn't there?"

For a while he didn't say anything, and neither Smuggler nor I said boo. Then he said softly: "I don't know," and he began telling me a story.

It was about a toad who had beautiful eyes. He was thirsty, and his feet had gotten very dirty. So now he was looking for a puddle that would be just about the right size for him to look at his beautiful eyes. He wanted to make sure that they were as beautiful as people said, and that it wasn't just empty flattery. He also wanted a drink, and to wash his feet, because he didn't dare to go home looking like that.

Finally he found a puddle, but there was hardly any water in it, only a wet spot.

The toad said to the puddle: "You've gone dry again?"

"Yes," the puddle said, "but it isn't my fault, be-

cause every day I have to give some of my water to the sea."

The toad felt sorry for the puddle. It was very unfair. *I thought.* The sea had so much water; why couldn't it give water to the puddle instead of the other way around? If I were a puddle, I wouldn't give a single drop to the sea. I would much rather make sure that the toad had enough water.

That's how I felt about it, I told my night daddy. He said that he had told me the story to explain why he wasn't always able to write, and that sometimes he felt like a dry puddle. It was a parable, he said.

"Like the stories in the Bible?"

"Yes, that's it."

"Am I the toad?" I asked. Because I pictured my-self as the toad and him as the puddle. But he didn't answer my question.

Yesterday was definitely not his day.

THE NIGHT DADDY

SOME NIGHTS Smuggler just insists on sitting on my head while I work, and I don't mind because he is just about the weight of my thoughts.

Smuggler is a treasure, and I'm very grateful to Jansson.

But Jansson had another treasure that he wanted me to look after. It was a plant, "the most extraordinary plant in the whole world," said Jansson. Everything Jansson owned, according to him, was the most extraordinary thing in the whole world. His ship is only one example. There was no other ship like it. He had the world's best scooter, too, the world's best radio, and of course the most marvelous owl in the world.

But to be perfectly honest, this flower didn't look like much, and when he began describing it, I got awfully bored. It was just an ordinary plant with green leaves and no sign of a flower. Besides, it looked kind of dusty. I almost asked how often it had to be dusted, but Jansson just kept raving on.

"This plant isn't like any other plant. It doesn't bloom very often or for very long, but when it does, it's the most beautiful flower in the whole world!

"It doesn't bloom for just anybody," he went on, sounding more and more like a preacher, "and it's temperamental so handle it as carefully as you would a baby. When it starts to bud, drop everything and watch over it day and night. Do that and I'll promise you'll thank me afterward."

Jansson had managed to make it sound quite exciting, so I took care of the plant as well as I could, but it never showed any signs of budding.

Time went by, and it continued to look as uninteresting as the day I got it. Jansson was romanticizing, I thought. He was just trying to put me on. "It doesn't bloom for just anybody," he had said, meaning me, of course, but I didn't care. I didn't think about the plant any more, but just kept on watering it out of habit.

Then one day what did I see? A bud! And I who had long ago given up on that dreary old vegetable!

Then I remember another thing Jansson had said: "The strangest thing about this plant is that it always blooms at night. By morning it's already faded. That's why you have to watch over it, especially at night—and that's why it's called Queen of the Night."

Well, I didn't take those remarks too seriously, because it was obvious that he was exaggerating. But the bud continued to grow—there was no denying that.

At first I decided not to bother with it. I was spending the nights at Julia's and wouldn't be around when it burst into bloom. It would already be fading when I came home in the morning, if one could believe Jansson, so there was no point in worrying about it. But for some reason I couldn't stop thinking about the plant; it kept haunting me.

One night when I left home the bud was enormous, and when I touched it, it felt alive, like a bird. It almost seemed as if there were a heart beating inside it, but it must have been my own pulse I was feeling. It was truly a fantastic flower.

I told Julia about it, what Jansson had said, and that it was called Queen of the Night. "Maybe the plant is blooming right this very minute," I said.

Julia became very upset. "Oh, no, we can't let that happen," she said. "Why didn't you bring her here?"

"I didn't know whether I ought to risk it. Maybe she doesn't travel well."

Julia looked as if she were about to burst into tears: "You mean to tell me she is to be left there all alone with no one to tell her how beautiful she is? What's the point of being beautiful if there's no one there to see you? And with a name like Queen of the Night. It's just too sad for words!"

"I think so, too," I said.

"Let's go and get her," cried Julia.

"Do you think we should?"

"We've got to!" she said.

"But what do you think your mother will say?"

We didn't have to worry about that, Julia said. Her mother would understand that we just couldn't leave the plant there to bloom all by herself. Her mother was a nurse, after all.

"But I'm not sure that it will bloom tonight," I said. "There's no way of knowing."

"Hurry up. I'm ready."

But it took quite a while before we got away. We had to take Smuggler along, and when we got outside we discovered it was raining, so we had to go back up for rain gear and a plastic cover for Smuggler's cage.

Then Julia decided that it would be a good idea to have something to eat in case we had to wait for the plant to bloom. There was nothing to eat at my house, so Julia made sandwiches for us. She also insisted that we bring along a record so that the Queen of the Night would have just the right kind of music to bloom by.

When we finally got off, we had quite a lot of baggage, and we must have looked funny in our rain capes—Julia's and mine were almost alike. I had a large basket in one hand and Smuggler's cage in the other. Julia was carrying the record and her grandfather's enormous umbrella, which she held over our heads. She had to keep her arm way up in the air because I was so much taller, but she didn't mind. It was quite an adventure to be out in the dark walking along the gleaming wet streets.

"This is almost like going to the moon," said Julia, lifting the umbrella still higher so that she was practically walking on tiptoe.

"It's not quite that far to my house," I said. "I live only a few blocks from here."

"Unknown places always seem far away—especially when it's dark."

I agreed, but still maintained that I didn't live that far away. "But why the moon?" I asked.

"*Because,*" she said. But for once I caught on and

realized that she didn't want me to accept that explanation, since she added: "Besides, I won't tell
you."

She wanted me to plead with her, so I did.

"*Please* tell me," I begged her.

Gradually she opened up. This is what she said: "Sometimes I have the feeling that you, Smuggler, and the Queen of the Night have come down from the moon, and that you just invented Jansson in order to seem more ordinary—more *earthly*."

"Do you like the idea of my coming from the moon?"

"I don't know."

"Would I be more interesting if I did?"

"No, I don't think that would make any difference," she said.

For a while she walked beside me thinking her own thoughts. Then suddenly she burst out with: "If you're going to disappear one day, I'd rather that you go to the moon than become someone else's night daddy."

Then it was my turn to walk beside her, thinking my own thoughts: "If I promise never to become anyone else's night daddy, and to come back to you, if I should disappear, wouldn't it be all right if I were a little more ordinary and earthly?"

Julia looked very serious as she said: "My mommy says one shouldn't make promises one can't keep."

"She's right. But if I tell you that I wouldn't ever

93

want to be anyone else's night daddy, will you believe me?"

Julia gave me a suspicious glance from under the umbrella.

"Do you have a lot of will power?"

"I think so."

"I do, too. My mother says it's hard as nails."

"Mine is as hard as iron."

"Then it's good enough for me."

Julia skipped, and the umbrella came down over my ears.

"Rain has such a nice cozy sound," she said, and Smuggler agreed because he hooted. The patter sounded nice on the umbrella.

Julia dragged her feet and seemed to want to prolong our walk as long as possible.

"Let's look at the shop windows," she said. "Don't you think that's fun?"

As a matter of fact, I do. Sometimes I stop in front of the displays just to feel how free I am. As I stood there looking at all the stuff I said aloud to myself: "How wonderful not to have to buy any of this!"

Julia looked at me as if I had suddenly lost my mind.

"What fun can there be in that?"

"Try it and you'll see for yourself. Let's stop and

look at the shoes. Look at them carefully. Would you really want to have any of them?"

"Yes, the green ones with the bow, or maybe the red ones. I can't decide which."

"But isn't it wonderful not to have to buy any of them? No one on earth, not even you yourself can force you to buy those shoes."

Julia looked puzzled. "What a funny idea. . . ."

"But a nice one," I said. "We'll just wave good-by to the shoes and leave. Good-by green shoes, good-by red shoes! This time you didn't catch us in your gaping jowls! Come, we'll sneak around this corner so they won't see where we're going."

By the time we got to the next display window, Julia was playing the game. "Let's look at these coats," she said. "How do you like the brown one with the shiny buttons?"

"Ugly."

"I don't agree with you, but never mind," said Julia. "Good-by, coat. You can just stay there with your sparkly buttons. You won't have to bother with us, and we won't have to bother with you. Good-by!"

We were getting very serious about our game, running forth and back across the street, looking at the display windows, feeling free as birds.

"Now it's my turn," I said. "Good evening, top hat. I'm so glad that your distinguished honorable self won't find a place on *my* head!"

"Because that's Smuggler's place," said Julia and giggled. Smuggler heard his name mentioned and had to chime in. He was playing the game in his own way.

Julia stopped again. "Hi there, sweet doll," she said with a lisp. "I'm sure your name is Sophie. You're trying to make an impression on us, but it won't work. We're leaving. Good night!"

"Isn't it a wonderful feeling to be able to get away?"

"Yes," said Julia, and meant it.

We walked along looking at this and that until we reached the park. "See that house between the trees on the other side of the park? That's where I live; Smuggler and I take walks here."

Julia suddenly remembered the Queen of the Night and began to run. I ran after her, and by the time we got to my house we were all out of breath.

My apartment is on the ground floor. Julia was amazed at how I opened the door. I never carry a key. This is a principle with me—the only one I have —and it's out of necessity. Keys have a way of disappearing, and then I can't get in!

But I've made a clever invention. Next to the

mailbox I've put a hook to which I've attached a long string. I open the mailbox, pull out the string, and at the end of it is the key to my apartment. I don't need a key to the front door because nobody ever bothers to lock it. It's an old house, and all the people in it are old—except me, of course.

Julia liked my trick with the key, and she promised not to tell a soul. She's the only one who knows about it.

(Maybe I shouldn't put this in our book, but I can always scratch it before it's printed. I'll ask Julia what she thinks. But no one could possibly know where I live, in what house, on what street, so there's no harm done, is there?)

"Well this is where I live," I said when we came in and I turned on the light. Then there was a terrible crash. It was Julia trying to make her way through all the books.

"What a mess," she said. "You can hardly get into this place."

I told her to hang her umbrella on the cow horn inside the door, and then I helped her to pull off her boots. She thought this was great fun.

"Where is the Queen of the Night?"

"She's over there in the corner."

Julia made a beeline for her, and my books flew all over the place.

"Oh, how beautiful you are!" she exclaimed.

"Is she blooming?" I said, trying to get out from under my rain gear.

"Not yet. How lucky that we got here in time!"

We somehow managed to clear a small space for us in front of the window and devoured the sandwiches. Smuggler was flying around and showing that he was master here. He pranced around and seemed very proud at having a guest. He usually doesn't have guests. How could they possibly fit into this room? But Julia is small enough to fit into the "cabin." We put our record on and played music for a night plant to bloom by. The bud seemed very much alive, but it was closed and didn't move.

"It doesn't look as if it will open tonight, either," I said.

I saw that Julia was getting sleepy—the sandwiches and the night-flower music were having their effect on her.

"You're tired, aren't you? We'd better get you home and to bed."

Julia rubbed her eyes.

"But suppose she bursts into bloom. Can't we take her along?"

"But maybe we shouldn't move her," I said.

"O.K. Then I'll stay."

But it was obvious that she was getting sleepy. It

was late, and I had no place to put her to bed. It seemed a good idea to take a taxi; then we could carry the plant safely.

"O.K.," I said. "We'll take it along. I'll call a taxi."

And off we went, Julia carrying the Queen of the Night, and I carrying Smuggler, of course.

But nothing happened that night. The Queen of the Night slept as soundly as we did.

JULIA

I JUST HAVE to write some more about Ulla and the others, although I hate to. They get nastier every day, and I can't stand them anymore. They never stop teasing me about my night daddy. They say that he isn't my real daddy, that they've never heard of anything so silly. Since he only comes at night, I must be dreaming, they say. . . .

It was stupid of me to tell them about him. I should have known that they would react that way. They never believe me; I'm the biggest liar in the world, according to them, and they say they're not going to let me get away with it. Then they say that if he does exist, he must exist in the daytime too. Did

I happen to know where he spent the day? Of course I said yes, because I do know. After all, I did go to his house the time we fetched the Queen of the Night.

"Can you find it again?" Ulla wanted to know.

I said I could, but I realized too late that I shouldn't have.

"Let's go," they said, because they still didn't believe me. I could have kicked myself for being led into that trap, but if I didn't take them there, it would be *proof* that I was a liar, they said.

I just couldn't show up there, especially not with them. What would he say? And what would he think of me? Besides, I want things to stay as they are; our nice evenings together give me enough to think about the whole next day. When I said that, they laughed even more.

They called him my nightpa, and that was horrible! And they said I'd invented him.

I don't want anyone to know where he lives, and what his room is like, and see the key and everything, because it's all very private.

But when they insisted, and kept on ridiculing me, I had to think of something. I didn't know what to do, so I agreed to call him up. I have his telephone number written down at home, although I know it by heart. Sometimes during the day I think about it, write it down on a piece of paper, and tear it up afterward. So although I know it, I won't tell it to a soul, because it's my secret.

We went to Ulla's house and phoned from there. When I dialed the number, I made sure no one saw me, although they tried to peek.

When I heard the phone ring at the other end, I was terrified. They were standing so close that they heard it, too, and just gaped. My heart was pounding and I was miserable.

It took him an endless time to answer. I was praying that he wouldn't be at home, but he was; and when he answered, I couldn't get a word out. And his voice sounded so strange and far away.

"Say something!" Ulla hissed in my ear.

But I still couldn't utter a word.

"Hello, who is it?" he said. But I still couldn't make a sound. He must have heard the girls chattering in the background.

Then Birgit took the receiver, tried to sound tough, and said:

"Hello, are you the nightpa?" and slammed down the receiver, laughing like mad.

I left them and ran all the way home.

I feel just rotten inside, and while I'm writing this, he's sitting in the living room being very quiet. He's probably wondering who called. Maybe he thinks it

is I who called him nightpa—but could he possibly think that? He hasn't mentioned it, and I don't want to bring it up in case he didn't hear them.

They were making such a racket that it was hard to hear anything. Maybe he thought that someone had dialed the wrong number.

What am I going to do? It's no fun to write when you're feeling like this, and when you're as mixed up as I am. I feel so stupid and ashamed to have dialed his secret and private number on Ulla's stupid telephone.

I'd like to have a telephone of silver—the kind they have in museums. If I could call him on one of those I'd know exactly what to say.

And on top of it all there was the Queen of the

Night who just wouldn't blossom. The bud hadn't developed since we moved the plant. We probably shouldn't have moved it. It was my fault; I had insisted that we bring it here, and the poor, poor plant probably stopped growing because of that.

I think I'll go and sit with him and Smuggler and do some knitting. I hate to knit more than anything, and that's why I have to do it. I'm so stupid I have to go against myself in everything. Otherwise I would do even more stupid things.

THE NIGHT DADDY

ONE NIGHT Julia behaved very strangely. She stayed by herself in her room. I think she was working at our book, but she wasn't at all in the usual good mood that she's in when she scribbles away. She seemed quiet and far away, and I didn't dare interrupt her.

I put on all the lights to try to get Smuggler to sleep, but it didn't work. He wasn't sleepy at all. He seemed to want to prove that he was a real night owl. He flew around, spreading his wings wide, but he finally calmed down and settled on my head. Only then was I able to do some reading.

Suddenly Julia burst in. She didn't say a word but just sat down and began knitting. I happen to know how much she hates knitting, so I tried to talk to her, but all she did was knit and knit and *knit!*

"It's cozy when you're reading and I'm knitting, isn't it?" she said.

When I asked her what she was making, she didn't answer but just sat there counting her stitches . . . purl two . . . knit one . . . purl two . . . knit one. I couldn't get a sensible word out of her. She seemed to be completely absorbed in her knitting, although I knew she was only pretending, because there's nothing she hates worse. She's told me that many times.

"Is it going to be a scarf?" I said, because that's what it looked like to me.

"No—purl two, knit one . . . purl two . . ."

Her knitting looked like a small, gradually elongating tube. It looked very mysterious, and it aroused my curiosity.

"Now I know what it is," I said. "You're knitting sox for a stork."

No? Well in that case I didn't have a clue.

Julia is usually such a chatterbox. Had I done something to make her act this way? Or was she just trying to be considerate so that I could read? No, there was definitely something wrong. I couldn't settle down to work, either. Julia had been behaving strangely for the past few days. What was the matter with her? She seemed to be fighting herself all the time. I just couldn't make her out.

I brought out some caramel lollipops, which she loves, and she looked very pleased. But suddenly her expression changed. She put down the lollipop, and said she didn't want it.

When she asked me if I wanted to play a game, and I said of course, she suddenly decided that she didn't want to. She put the game away and disappeared into her room, looking very unhappy.

Had I said something wrong or hurt her in some way? I wracked my brains but couldn't remember anything that could have upset her. Besides, she would have told me, for she isn't shy, and we've always been completely honest with each other—that's the way it has to be.

It's awful when people can't communicate anymore, and finally I couldn't stand it any longer. I just had to ask Julia if she was mad at me.

But she only shook her head, and her knitting needles clicked louder than ever.

"But tell me what's the matter?"

"I'm disciplining myself."

"Oh. Do you think others have done such a bad job on you?"

She thought that over while scratching her head with a knitting needle.

"I'm the only one who knows how to handle me," she said solemnly. "And you should never expect other people to help bring you up, because they have their own selves to educate."

I thought about that and decided it was time I started on my own self-discipline, which I had long neglected.

She must have been thinking about me, although she didn't say so straight out. But at my age it isn't easy to know where to start, and I told her so.

"Yes," was all she said, leaving me to figure out what she meant, while her knitting needles clicked away.

"I think one ought to be able to practice a little self-discipline without making such a fuss about it," I said.

"Yes," said Julia again.

Then she began with her "knits" and "purls" again, and there was no way of getting to her.

"I'm going to make some tea," I said. "Would you like some before you go to bed?"

She quickly looked up, gave me an enthusiastic "Yes," and then went right back to her knitting: "knit one . . . *no thank you* . . . purl two," she said.

"Julia, you're not counting right. You said purl *two*. 'Purl' means a backward stitch, doesn't it? There's only one of those around here, and that's you!"

"Yes, I know, and that's why I'm disciplining myself," she said, looking deadly serious.

"But aren't you being a bit hard on yourself?"

"Yes. . . ."

"Do you have to do it that way?"

"Yes."

"That's too bad because we can't have a nice time together when you're working so hard on your upbringing," I said and sighed.

"Why can't you make your own tea?"

Of course I could, but that wasn't the point. Julia gave me a dark look and said in an angry voice:

"When I say 'no' to myself I mean it. Don't interfere with my self-discipline. I happen to be spoiled."

"You are?"

"Yes, I am."

"Who spoiled you?"

"You did! You're good to me."

I knew she meant it, but the way she said it was not flattering. Besides, how can you spoil someone by being good to them? What was she trying to say? I didn't understand her at all.

"I mean," said Julia, and this time she sounded like her old good-natured self, "that if you say 'no' to yourself then the people whom you love don't have to do it for you. If I say 'no' to myself you can keep on spoiling me. I would like that very much. I'll do the job on myself, and you won't have to do it. Do you understand what I mean?"

I nodded, not knowing what to say, and all I could do was to ask her if she didn't want a cup of tea after all.

She shook her head.

"I heard a program about bringing up children. The worst thing you could possibly do is to give in to nagging," she said and looked very serious.

"Have I been nagging at you?"

"No, but I nag at myself. You should hear what it sounds like inside me! I keep on telling myself that I want some tea. I say 'no' to myself, but then I start nagging at myself all over again. I have to say 'no' to myself at least a thousand times. It's hard to do, believe me. I get so sick of all this nagging!"

"Well, then, maybe you'd better go to bed," I said. She looked tired and I really didn't know what to do next. I thought that it might be that she had this self-discipline idea because she was so tired. And I had a bad conscience because she had been getting to bed much too late. We have such a good time that we forget all about bedtime.

But when I said she had to go to bed, she said that was a different matter, and all of a sudden she was her same old self.

"No, I'm not going to bed," she said very firmly.

"Apparently your efforts at self-discipline don't always work," I said.

She looked at me with a quiet, if somewhat superior, air.

"Can't you let me talk to myself first? I haven't had a chance to do it yet. I can't obey myself before I've given myself an order, can I?"

"Well, when do you intend to do that?"

"I'll see. First I have to finish this row. And then

I'll decide. I've told you that you don't need to worry about taking care of me."

"O.K." I said, and went out to the kitchen to make some tea, and some warm milk and honey for Julia. I thought that the milk might be more in keeping with her self-discipline.

When I came back she had gone to her room, but she called me.

"I've gone to bed, *finally*."

"That's great," I said. "But I brought you a cup of hot milk. Do you think you're allowed to drink that?"

"Is there any honey in it?"

"Yes."

"How much?"

"A heaping teaspoon."

"Yes, that's all right. Honey is good for me."

"Well, that's what I thought, too."

I brought her the milk and sat at the foot of her bed while she drank it. All of a sudden she said:

"Nobody believes that you exist. Did you know that?"

"No, but it's very sad not to exist."

"They think I've invented you, and that I'm telling lies, and that you aren't real."

"Who are *they*?"

"The kids at school—Ulla and her crowd. They go into fits of laughter and say there's no such thing as a night daddy, and that I've invented you because I don't have a real father. And when I said that you're real, even though you only come at night, they said I was dreaming. But I don't want to have a real father, so there!"

She was tilting the cup at a dangerous angle, so I took it and began to spoon-feed her.

"One spoon for mommy, one spoon for your night daddy," I said.

She laughed.

"They say that a real daddy is around *all the time*, not only at night. But what's so special about that? You and I have so much more fun. I don't care how real their daddies are, but they just can't tell me you don't exist. 'You have crazy fantasies, just like old ladies,' they say. Then I fly into a rage."

"Let them think whatever they like. The important thing is that *we* know."

Julia didn't say anything but took the cup from me and carefully scraped out all the honey that was left at the bottom. Then she sucked the spoon as if it were a lollipop.

"Julia," I said, "pinch my arm so that I know if we're dreaming or not."

She laughed and pinched me hard.

"Ouch!" I cried. "There! Now do you believe I'm real?"

"Those kids still wouldn't believe me."

"Why should you care what they think?"

Julia was furious. That was the most stupid thing she'd ever heard, she said.

"You mean they should be allowed to believe that you don't exist? That may be all right with you, but not with me."

I tried to say that there wasn't much we could do about it. People believe what they want to believe. Whatever we did would be wrong. "Some things work themselves out—most of them do," I said.

"I'm *sure* there's something we can do about it, and I'm going to find the answer! I'm going to find a way to prove that you exist!"

"I don't care what people think about me," I said, making another try to reason with her. "They can believe I don't exist if they want to. It doesn't bother me!"

She looked at me with cold, furious eyes.

"They don't believe that Smuggler exists either," she said.

Then of course I had to react.

"That's different," I said. "No, we can't stand for that. We have to do something!"

"There you are! Now maybe you can understand why I'm so mad. 'How childish,' they say. But Smuggler is hardly childish, is he?" At this Smuggler protested furiously. He understands everything that's said, and he's far from childish. What a terrible thing to say!

"No, you couldn't possibly say that about him," I said, very upset, "Smuggler who is such a full-feathered adult!"

When Julia heard how upset we were—both Smuggler and I—she calmed down. She began yawning so that her eyes watered. Then she lay down and I tucked her in.

"This business of self-discipline is a big job, and the knitting, and all the rest . . ." she said.

"I can imagine. Now we're going to sleep, all three of us so that we can muster enough strength to prove that we exist."

"Thank you," said Julia, practically asleep.

JULIA

I THINK I HAD just fallen asleep when I dreamt that Smuggler flew in and excitedly hooted that the plant was about to burst into bloom! "But Smuggler, you're not a plant," I said. "How can you tell?"

He kept right on hooting, of course, because he is the world's most stubborn creature.

"Take a whiff of me," he said, and I did. He smelled of vanilla. What had he been up to this time? Had he been in the pantry and knocked something down? Or had he eaten something that wasn't good for him? There was a strong fragrance around him, as he kept hopping around and flapping his wings.

"I've blossomed! I've blossomed!" he cried, and felt that he had really done something great. Then he flew off, and I woke up.

The whole room still smelled of vanilla—it was a lovely smell.

Then suddenly I remembered the Queen of the Night! I flew out of bed and got there just in time. I put on a light—not the ceiling light of course, but a candle—and it began to open slowly, so slowly that you could hardly see it. But I saw it! It was as if it were slowly waking up and feeling its way.

Smuggler was awake and also saw what was happening. We didn't know how we were going to wake my night daddy without disturbing the Queen of the Night. Luckily, he woke up by himself. He stirred around in bed and mumbled: "Where am I? Am I dreaming? What kind of a smell is that?"

He took a couple of whiffs and then lay there sniffing and making very funny noises. He was so funny that I couldn't help laughing. Then he sat up, scratched his head, and tried to put his feet in his slippers. Suddenly he flew out of bed and began looking around.

"But the whole place smells of *vanilla!*" he yelled, as if the house were on fire.

Then he saw the plant.

"Now aren't you surprised?" I whispered, trying

to keep from laughing out loud as he leapt across
the room in two enormous bounds.

"This is fantastic! When did it happen?"

"Don't talk so loud. You have to whisper! We
mustn't frighten the plant."

The Queen of the Night looked so alive and
trembling, just like an animal waking up, that when
you looked at her you thought: "She's going to move
any minute!" I wouldn't have been at all surprised if

she had turned toward me and nodded. My night daddy was so excited he couldn't stop talking.

"Jansson was right after all!" he exclaimed. "And I thought he was just bragging! I was just dreaming about Jansson," he said. "It was a fantastic dream."

It was very strange that we had both had similar dreams just at the moment when the Queen of the Night was bursting into bloom.

"What was your dream about?" I whispered.

"I dreamt I was somebody's crazy invention that had gone wrong," he said slowly. "It was as if I were lost and they were trying to find me, and . . ."

Then he told me about his dream and I'm going to ask him to write it down, because I don't think I could. I only hope he will. I'm going to ask him right away!

(He agreed to do it, and he is starting right now!)

THE NIGHT DADDY

IN YOUR DREAMS you can become just about anything. I was a crazy invention that had gone wrong. I had no idea where I came from or where I was going. I just knew that I was lost. And it didn't bother me in the least that a crazy invention might look strange. But that's what I was, and I couldn't care less.

"They" were out looking for me, but who "they" were I hadn't the faintest idea. To Julia "they" were Ulla and her gang, but I wasn't so sure. Since I never saw "them," it could have been just about anybody. I just got the word that "they" were looking for me. That made no sense at all because none of "them"

knew what a crazy invention looked like, so therefore they couldn't possibly know where to find me.
In order to find me they would have had to invent
me themselves. If they had, none of them seemed
willing to admit it.

Well, it was all very confused, the way dreams
usually are. Julia was in it, too, and she was mad at
me.

"You could at least tell me who invented you,"
she said.

"I thought *you* did," I said. "I was hoping so.
Everything would have been so much simpler then."

But that made her even angrier.

"I'd never do a thing like that. I have enough trouble with my own inventions."

And that's true enough.

(When Julia read this, she exclaimed at this
point: "I'd never be able to invent somebody like
you!")

Well, I felt very lost in that dream. It's no fun having people hunting for you. And on top of everything, Julia was mad at me.

But then Jansson, the sea captain, turned up and
stuck his head out of the chimney of his old ship.
The smoke was rising around his ears, but that
didn't seem to bother him a bit because he looked
very much in command of everything. He glared at

me and claimed that I was *his* invention, and that I was the best invention the world had ever seen!

Then it was my turn to get mad.

"Now look here, Jansson, you can't fool me," I said. And the moment I said it I knew what had happened. *I had invented myself!* That's why nobody knew me and nobody could find me, no matter how hard they looked. How clever of me! That was the only possible answer. What a wonderful feeling it is to find the answer to a problem!

I couldn't wait to tell Julia that it was I who had invented myself. But she only shook her head, and then she said something astounding:

"That's just what I would expect of you, but now you won't get any vanilla sauce with your dessert!"

I was convinced she had gone off her rocker, but at that moment I woke up and actually smelled vanilla!

Julia was standing by the window holding a lighted candle, and Smuggler was sitting next to her. The candle was shining on the Queen of the Night, which had finally burst into bloom. It was a beautiful sight! For a moment I thought I was sleeping again in the midst of another dream.

The Queen of the Night was a fantastic plant—unbelievable.

JULIA

WE DON'T READ each other's diaries, but he promised that I could read about his dream right away because I couldn't stand to wait. It's very strange, isn't it?

To me the Queen of the Night was very *real*, but in an *unreal* way.

Now I have to write about what happened after that. It's hard for me, but it would be still harder for my night daddy because he probably still hasn't gotten over it. I felt so sorry for him, and I feel so terrible when I think about it.

We stood there for a long time looking at the Queen of the Night—she seemed to grow before our very eyes. We didn't want to leave her, so we played music for her—special records, which we had chosen beforehand, for the moment when she burst into bloom, night-flower music.

Then my night daddy said:

"The smell of vanilla is very strong. . . ."

I thought so, too. It almost made me dizzy, as if I were caught up in a dream.

"It's really gone to my head," he said. "Maybe we ought to open the window?"

It was a relief, and the smell was even more delicious when it blended with the fresh night air. We kept on inhaling it, and he closed his eyes because it was so marvelous.

Then there was a flapping of wings over our heads.

It took us a few seconds to realize what was going on. Then I screamed:

"Smuggler is flying out through the window! Stop him!"

But there was no stopping Smuggler. He was already flying over the rooftop towards the church tower. We kept on calling him, but he didn't pay the slightest attention to us.

At first we could see him because he was a dark spot in the sky, but then we lost sight of him. He disappeared. He didn't even hoot or make his tjop-

ping sound. He just kept on flying, and wouldn't
listen to our calls.

It's hard to write about this, and I don't want to
think about it. It isn't that I'm mad at Smuggler for
flying away; it's only that I feel so sorry for my night
daddy. We stayed up almost the whole night talking, and I told him a silly story because I couldn't
think of anything to make him feel better—nothing that he would really believe, and nothing that
wouldn't make him feel still sadder. There wasn't
much that I could say.

O.K., I thought, Smuggler is gone and that's that.
But out loud I said:

"Smuggler can take care of himself."

It was a very sad night. We left the window open, but he didn't come back. It was dark—there was no moon—and the fragrance of vanilla floated in the air all night long.

THE NIGHT DADDY

JULIA INSISTED on writing about Smuggler's disappearance. I don't know why she felt she had to do it. I felt so sorry for her! She couldn't sleep that night. She was waiting for Smuggler and just kept on calling his name, thinking that he would be back, that he was only playing a trick on us. I thought so, too.

It was a terrible night. I don't know who worried me more—Julia or Smuggler.

Then I became alarmed. Suppose something were to happen to Smuggler! He wasn't used to the life out there. How would he manage to get food? Then I became annoyed with myself for worrying, and annoyed with Smuggler for making me worry, and ended up by being angry with myself. I tried to keep calm for Julia's sake, because I had to calm her down. She was very much upset and kept on defending Smuggler as if she thought I was angry with him. But I wasn't: only sad and trying to figure out why he did it.

"He probably wants to show us that he can stand on his own feet," said Julia. "Maybe he wants to be free."

"But I thought he was happy with me!"

"Of course he was. He has had a wonderful life! But you're not an owl, you know, and there's nothing you can do about that."

Julia often brought that up. It's true that I'm not an owl, but that can't have come as a great surprise to Smuggler—he surely must have discovered that a long time ago. That was no reason for him to fly away just now! If he had wanted to escape, he had lots of opportunities. I haven't tried to stop him; at home I used to leave the window open all day.

"In the *daytime*, yes," said Julia. "But not at night. The night is his time, you know."

"But he was in the process of changing his habits, wasn't he?"

"Haven't you read anything except books about stones?" said Julia.

I didn't follow her. What did that have to do with it? Of course I had read about other things, but mostly about stones. "What do you mean?" I said.

"You should have been reading about owls. I have. I've read lots of books about animals. I began when I first met Smuggler."

"You like animals a lot, don't you?"

"Yes, but Smuggler most of all."

For a long time we sat there, each with our own thoughts. After a while Julia said:

"Don't worry. Smuggler can take care of himself."

"You really think so?"

"I *know* he can," said Julia.

"He'll probably come back." I said that for Julia's sake because I had begun to have my doubts. If I could only understand why he did it! Then something occurred to me. Could it be that he was jealous of the Queen of the Night—the way children sometimes are when a new baby appears? In some ways he is like a child. After all, we were standing there, our eyes glued to the plant and not paying any attention to him. Maybe that was it! Maybe he felt rejected!

Julia also thought it odd that he had decided to take off just then. She agreed that it could have something to do with the plant.

"There was something very mysterious about the Queen of the Night," she said. "We felt it, too, although we're only human beings. So we can only guess how a creature of the night like Smuggler would react to her."

She was lost in thought for a while, and then wondered out loud whether Smuggler might have been under a spell. Maybe he was a bewitched prince, or a professor, or someone like that, who had been changed into an owl because he was too wise. Maybe the Queen of the Night was the only one who could help him. When she blossomed and Smuggler inhaled the fragrance, then hokus pokus, the spell was broken and he could go back home to his princess (or his wife, if he were a professor) who was going around crying and waiting for him. Maybe Jansson was a magician—but not an evil one, because that's why he had asked me to take care of Smuggler and the Queen of the Night—so that there would be a happy ending.

"Now do you understand?" she asked.

"You've been reading a lot of fairy tales," I said.

She looked a bit miffed.

"Maybe," she said. "But don't you believe in fairy tales?"

"Of course I do. They're often more real than

reality; reality can really play bad tricks on people; I've noticed that through the years."

"There you are!" cried Julia. "Then why do you keep on contradicting me?"

"I keep on thinking about Jansson. He was a typical sea captain and didn't look like a magician at all."

But Julia remarked that I couldn't know what a magician looked like. "That isn't written in people's faces," she said. And besides, Jansson had probably changed himself into someone else.

"I've always thought there was something funny about him since the first time you mentioned him," she said.

She was probably right. Just the fact that he got me a place to live—these days you really have to be a magician to do that!

"That's exactly what I mean!" said Julia.

I asked her if she didn't think that we ought to look for Smuggler—perhaps he had become a professor now.

But of course that only made the whole thing worse. It wouldn't be easy to get a professor to admit that he had spent some time being an owl. Maybe he wouldn't even remember. People usually lose their memory after having been bewitched.

But Julia impatiently waived that argument aside.

Of course we had to look for Smuggler! We couldn't give up. We had to know what happened to him. After all, he might turn out to be an ordinary owl, she said.

I was glad that Julia also wanted to hunt for him, because I had to know if he needed something or wanted us. Julia and I were his only friends; we understood him—but not completely of course. Since it's so hard to understand human beings—because it is—then it's ever so much harder to understand animals.

I said this to Julia because I wanted her to know that I was finally beginning to realize that I wasn't an owl. Julia seemed very pleased; she only nodded but didn't say anything.

At daybreak we went out to look for Smuggler. Julia called her mother at the hospital and told her what had happened. Julia took Smuggler's cage along in case he should be tired and would want to have a place to sleep in peace after his adventures.

At that hour there was hardly a soul around. We ran into a woman selling newspapers, but when we asked if she had seen an owl, she looked cross and didn't answer. She apparently thought that we were having fun with her.

I kept on calling Smuggler. My voice echoed

through the quiet streets and sounded strange and lonely. It gave me an eerie feeling somehow. But Julia stepped in at this point and told me to stop calling.

"It sounds crazy; you musn't call Smuggler like that! People might think that you're very strange!" she said.

"It wasn't I who named him Smuggler," I said. "Besides, what's wrong with being called Smuggler?"

But she maintained that we couldn't go around the streets at dawn calling his name because people would think that there was something wrong. Besides, I was waking up everybody; people were looking out of their windows and laughing. I hadn't noticed, but now that Julia mentioned it, I saw some curtains being cautiously moved to one side.

"What do you want me to call him then?" I asked.

"We have to look for him—not call him," she said.

But where should we start? I was feeling more and more discouraged; Smuggler could have flown off in any direction. To me it seemed hopeless. But Julia didn't think he had flown too far away. She was convinced he was sleeping in a tree nearby.

"He could just as easily be sitting on some roof," I said.

"First things first. We'll have to search the roof-tops later."

I went along with that. She was being very brave and showing great self-control, but I sensed how miserable she was; and I felt so sorry for her. We had to find Smuggler fast—for Julia's sake.

JULIA

Looking for Smuggler was harder than I had thought. We were out all morning, and then we went to my house for breakfast, because you get hungry when you're on a search party. Mommy called my teacher and I got permission to stay home from school.

Then we went out again. I was worried because I knew how he felt, although I didn't let on. The hardest thing is to try to console someone. I know that, because I don't believe them when they try to console me. Sometimes they just try to fool children; I've been through that many times, and I didn't want to do it to my night daddy. He has to be able to trust me as I trust him. He doesn't try to fool anyone, not when he's trying to make me feel better, and not otherwise either. I knew that the minute I saw him. He's never told me a lie. Almost everyone else has, and it's a nasty feeling because you can't tell them you know they're lying. Then you feel older than they, and that's not a very nice feeling— not the same as when you're playing grownups. I think grownups ought to be grownups and not act like children. They can *pretend* to be children, the way my night daddy does when he is fooling around, although he is a grownup. I wouldn't ever want another night daddy, and I'm always going to tell mine the truth.

Nothing could have happened to Smuggler. Owls always get by, even tame ones. Some wild animals can't fend for themselves if they have been in captivity and are suddenly given their freedom. But owls are different—they can take care of themselves. I read that in a book—that's how I know.

Now I want to tell what happened next. A lot of kids followed us, acting stupid and making nasty remarks. They had heard us calling Smuggler and began mimicking us. I turned around and saw a few of my classmates—the meanest of them—who had said that my night daddy was an invention. Ulla was with them, and in a way I was glad they were there so that they would all be convinced that he existed— Ulla too.

We walked slowly so that they could catch up with us, and they acted stupid and silly as they passed us.

"So, you're playing hooky," said Ulla in passing.

I told her that the teacher had given me permission to look for Smuggler; they hadn't believed that Smuggler existed either. And their faces got *that* long—especially Ulla's—when my night daddy told them who he was. They became all confused, and giggled. But when he began describing Smuggler and asking if they had seen him, they forgot to put on their silly act. When he talked to them they behaved like human beings—even Ulla. But they hadn't seen Smuggler.

Then we went off in different directions.

It was almost dark and still no sign of Smuggler.

"We'll soon find him. We have to keep on looking," I said.

I was sure that we would end up by finding him, but I wasn't so sure that we could get him to come home with us—he's an owl after all. We continued to remind ourselves of that.

My night daddy had to go to his house to see if there was any mail, so I waited outside.

Now darkness had fallen, and I felt it especially

because I was alone. How could we find Smuggler now when we hadn't been able to all day? We had covered the whole area, and even been to the woods outside town.

He had probably been tired and asleep all day, but now that it was dark he would be wide awake. If only he wouldn't fly too far away now that he was rested!

All of a sudden I heard a lot of running and shouting. Despite the darkness I was able to recognize a few of my classmates, but Ulla wasn't among them. I saw Birgit and Kerstin and a couple of the boys who belonged to that crowd. They had never been nice, but now they were anxious to help. When they saw me they cried:

"Your Smuggler is sitting in a tree over there! We saw him!"

I didn't quite believe them, and besides I was still alone, so I didn't answer.

"Honestly," said one of the boys, "I saw him fly over there."

They ran ahead of me to show the way, and I followed, afraid that Smuggler had already flown off.

When we got there, Ulla was standing under the tree keeping an eye on him so that she could tell us in which direction he had gone, in case he should take off. It was kind of her (she can still be my best friend!). She was smiling—even though both Birgit and Kerstin were there and I didn't have my night daddy beside me. Maybe everything had changed for the better, so I ran over to her. She pointed to the tree.

"There! Behind that big branch!" she said.

"Where? I don't see him!"

"No, not there! Higher up!"

They were all pointing in different directions, and I got all confused. Luckily Smuggler moved, and then I saw him.

"Smuggler come here! It's only Julia!"

But although I kept on calling him, he didn't make a move. He didn't even hoot, but his eyes glittered.

Then my night daddy came running and calling me because he couldn't see me in the crowd.

"We've found Smuggler. Hurry!" I cried.

He ran still faster and looked so happy. But Smuggler still wouldn't come down, although we both called him. He just sat there quietly and didn't hoot once.

We were a bit worried. It could be that he was afraid of the crowd and all the children standing below. But we couldn't chase them away, especially

not Ulla and the kids who had found him, and who were hopefully going to be nice from now on.

Finally my night daddy and a couple of the boys went off to get a ladder, and I stayed behind to watch Smuggler. Ulla was standing right next to me. We were afraid that he would fly away when they raised the ladder.

Nobody moved while my night daddy slowly climbed up, quietly calling Smuggler.

When he was very close he reached out for him, but Smuggler flew into the air. I felt myself getting weak. But the next moment he landed on my shoulder, and from there he flew to my night daddy's head, where he sat quietly while my night daddy climbed down the ladder.

Smuggler stayed in the same position all the way through the park. The crowd was following us as we headed toward my night daddy's house; it was closer than mine, and we wanted to be alone with Smuggler.

As soon as we got inside the door, Smuggler was almost his old self, although he seemed to have something on his mind. But he hooted and then did one of his tricks: he flew over to the copper kettle and pushed away the lid. Then he hid inside it, and we had to turn the kettle upside down to shake him out. It was his favorite game, and the kettle was also his hiding place when he had gotten into mischief. For him, it was like standing in the corner.

But this time he hadn't done anything foolish; my night daddy didn't think so, either.

"Smuggler is just like his old self," he said. "I thought all along that he was too smart to be a professor."

Smuggler bounced back and forth between us like a ball. He seemed to be happy and pleased with himself.

I thought it was because he was back home again. He may have flown away because he wanted to be in his own house and not in mine. But my night daddy didn't agree, and when Smuggler had calmed down and was sitting in front of him on the table, my night daddy asked him:

"What's the matter Smuggler? Why did you leave us? We're so fond of you." They looked each other squarely in the eye. "Do you want to be free? Is that what you really want?"

Smuggler hooted. It almost sounded as if he were saying yes. I hadn't imagined it, because we both heard it.

"What do you think, Julia?"

"Yes, he wants to be free, but . . ."

"But what?"

"He also wants to stay with you."

We looked at each other and didn't know what to do. It was a difficult decision, both for us and for Smuggler. And Smuggler was sitting there with a hopeful look that we couldn't quite interpret.

"Look at me Smuggler! I don't want to make you a prisoner. Of course you can have your freedom!"

Smuggler again answered us. He seems to understand just about everything.

"O.K." my night daddy kept on saying to himself.

That was all he said. He was thinking, and so was I.
For a while we didn't say a word. Smuggler was also
thinking. Then we had a good idea. If we opened
the window now when it was dark, we would soon
know whether Smuggler would stay or fly away.
Then he could decide for himself. He could *choose!*

That was the best solution. My night daddy got
up and opened the window. We were on pins and
needles and hardly dared to breathe.

Smuggler just sat there and didn't make a move—
except for his eyes, which glittered. We didn't say a
word but waited. The curtain fluttered, and the
fresh air came streaming in. From the park came the

sound of the wind rustling the leaves, and the sky was filled with stars. Smuggler still didn't move. He probably wanted to stay after all. Just as we were making signs to each other, he lifted his wings and came over to me. For a while he sat on my arm, and then he flew over to my night daddy and settled on his head.

"Do you think I need to collect my thoughts, Smuggler?" he asked.

It almost sounded as if Smuggler were laughing. He hooted loudly and gaily, and then flew right out the window. We ran over to look, and there he was, flying back and forth. He was hooting at us, flapping his wings, and doing all kinds of tricks.

"You're free Smuggler! You can fly wherever you want to, you rascal!"

But Smuggler came back once more. He flew back into the room, circled around several times, and then flew off again. We shouted after him: "If you want to come back and visit us sometime Smuggler, we'll be very glad to see you. We'll always leave the window open. You can sleep here whenever you feel like it—if it's cold or raining. And if you want food, you know where to find it."

We called after him the way mothers sometimes call after their children when they are about to embark on an adventure.

Smuggler hooted in reply before taking off across the park.

"Isn't he beautiful in the air! Aren't you glad that he's able to manage on his own?"

But my night daddy didn't look very happy, although he said he was, for Smuggler's sake. But I know that for himself he was sad.

"We'll get over it!"

"Sure we will."

Then we turned our thoughts to how happy we would be when Smuggler came to visit us. I'm sure he'll come around often. I could tell by the way he looked at us.

"You'll call me up and say that Smuggler has arrived and that I have to come right away, and I'll be over like a shot. And sometimes Smuggler might come to my house, and then I'll call you and tell you to hurry over."

I think we'll be much happier now that we know he's free and can be with other owls. My night daddy thought so, too. He laughed and said that he was a bit sentimental about Smuggler, but he would try some self-discipline on himself. But I said he didn't need to, and he was very pleased about that.

Then we went to the park and got some frankfurters and ice cream. While we were there, we thought we heard someone flitting around and hoot-

ing above us. We realized that it was Smuggler playing a game. We played with him, and hoped it would
never stop.

"Just keep on playing," he seemed to say. And
that's exactly what we did.

THE NIGHT DADDY

OF COURSE I did feel a little sad seeing Smuggler fly
away. I must admit I hadn't really meant to let
him go again, but now I'm happy for his sake. He
flies so beautifully. He's such a splendid owl. He'll
get on well with the other owls and make lots of
friends. I feel proud of Smuggler.

And of Julia. My night daughter.

Julia doesn't know yet what made me decide to
let Smuggler go free. It was something she said, and
if she hadn't said those words, who knows what
would have happened.

She said, "Now you've got me, you know. You

didn't before, not that I'm anything special to have, perhaps. . . ."

I couldn't think of an answer when she said that, and I can't find anything to say now, either. It's as if no words would do. But if only she knew. . . .

I think I did say, "You really are my night daughter. . . ."

And then Julia said, "Then we've got to *prove* it."

"What?"

"That you're my night daddy. And I'm your night child. And that night daddies are *real* daddies. That they *exist*."

"That's quite a lot to show all at once," I said. "And besides, Ulla and the others have seen me."

"*They* have but . . ."

"Do you think they're nicer now?"

She looked at me uncertainly.

"Will it *last?*" she asked.

Julia is really bright.

"Well," I said, "I don't know. They probably won't be so mean any more. But it's better to be prepared in case they are nasty again."

"That doesn't matter," answered Julia. "Anyway, now they *know* . . ."

"Isn't that enough?" I asked. "That they know?"

Julia shook her head and looked at me intently.

"There are so many others. People don't believe it

if you say that there are different kinds of daddies. We've got to say it so *everyone* understands."

Sometimes I think really slowly and stupidly. I knew that this was important to Julia, but I didn't understand quite how we were going to carry it out.

Then she explained, "We'll write a book about us."

A book? But I'm already writing one. The one about stones. Another book? Write two books? How could I? No. . . .

As I say, my mind works slowly.

"I think this could be our secret," I told her. But now I see clearly that I knew better when I said it.

"No, impossible," said Julia. "Then they'd only think I *invented* you. Or they might also say that I *dreamed* it."

"Sometimes I feel I'm an invention," I tried, another way.

"Then you can only do what your inventor invents for you to do," said Julia. "Isn't that right?"

"Okay, then I want to be a dream instead."

"How impractical you are. A dream only gets to do what the dreamer dreams."

"Well, that could be great. If *you* were the dreamer."

Then Julia looked at me severely, and she was quite right when she said I was only offering a lot of dumb excuses and lazy flattery which didn't suit me. And then she reminded me of that strange dream which she had insisted I write down, when I dreamed I was my own invention.

Her parting shot was, "Anyway, you're your own dream. You're not *mine*."

"Then I'm not a dream daddy?" I asked, trying to make everything cozy again.

Failed. She turned her back and wouldn't answer me.

Then she said, "I'm *dead serious*."

"I know you are," I said. "I'm sorry."

Then I walked off alone and mulled over the whole thing. A couple of days passed. One evening when Julia sat at home writing so hard that her pen almost glowed red hot from the speed, I went in to see her.

I stopped in the doorway, stood there a while silently. I lit my pipe.

Then, looking up at me, she said, "I'm writing the book anyway, and you can do whatever you like."

"O.K., I'll write it, too," I said.

She looked really happy, but didn't answer right away. Then she looked up slyly.

"For Smuggler's sake?" she asked.

"That's just it," I answered. "So no one will doubt that he exists. I can't take that."

"We've got to write about everything, all the way from the beginning, all together. . . ."

"Shall we tell about the sign, too?" I asked. " 'Private Property! Don't Disturb! Forbidden!' "

Julia was silent for an unusually long time. Then she said,

"If it's absolutely necessary . . . O.K."